62のソネット+36

谷川俊太郎

集英社文庫

62のソネット＋36

目次

I

1 木蔭 18
2 憧れ 20
3 帰郷 22
4 今日 24
5 偶感 26
6 朝1 28
7 朝2 30
8 笑い 32
9 困却 34
10 知られぬ者 36

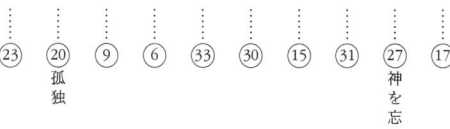

⑰
㉗ 神を忘る
㉛
⑮
㉚
㉝
⑥
⑨
⑳ 孤独
㉓

11 沈黙 38		
12 廃墟 40		
13 今 42		
14 野にて 44		
15 鋳型 46		
16 朝3 48		
17 始まり 50		
18 鏡 52		
19 ひろがり 54		
20 心について 56		
21 歌 58		
22 姿について 60		

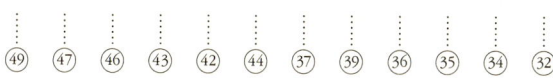

㊾ ㊼ ㊻ ㊸ ㊷ ㊹ ㊲ ㊴ ㊱ ㉟ ㉞ ㉜

23 雲 62

24 夢 64

Ⅱ

25 〈世界の中で私が身動きする〉 68

26 〈ひとが私に向かって歩いてくる〉 70

27 〈地球は火の子供で身重だ〉 72

28 〈眠ろうとすると〉 74

29 〈私は思い出をひき写している〉 76

30 〈私は言葉を休ませない〉 78

31 〈世界の中の用意された椅子に座ると〉 80

32 〈時折時間がたゆたいの演技をする〉 82

㊵ ㊶

㊾ ㊽ ㊼ ㊻ ㊺ ㊹ ㊸ ㊷

33 （私は近づこうとした） 84

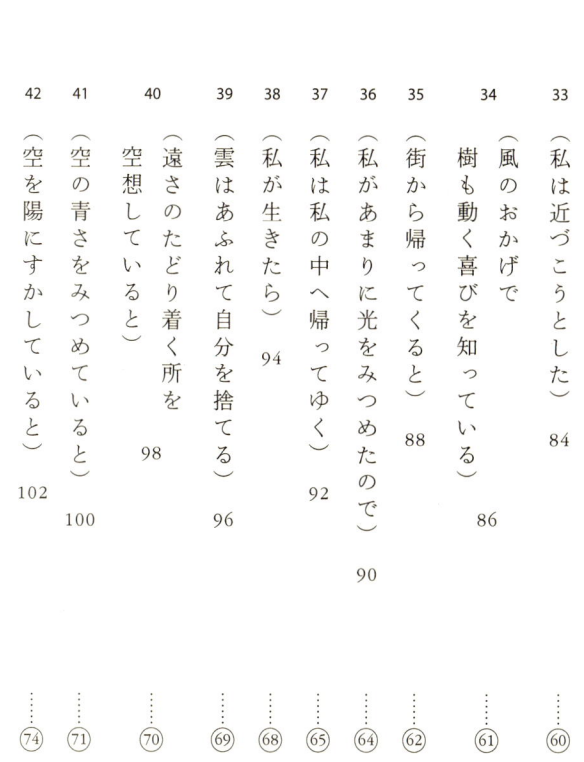

34 （風のおかげで
樹も動く喜びを知っている） 86

35 （街から帰ってくると） 88

36 （私があまりに光をみつめたので） 90

37 （私は私の中へ帰ってゆく） 92

38 （私が生きたら） 94

39 （雲はあふれて自分を捨てる） 96

40 （遠さのたどり着く所を
空想している） 98

41 （空の青さをみつめていると） 100

42 （空を陽にすかしていると） 102

60
61
62
64
65
68
69
70
71
74

III

43 〈あふれた空の光を〉 104 ㊅

44 〈私は闘士であったから〉 106 ㊆

45 〈風が強いと〉 108 ㊆

46 〈若い陽がひととき〉 110 ㊆

47 〈時が曇った夜空に滲みてゆく〉 112 ㊆

48 〈私たちはしばしば生の影が〉 114 ㊇

49 〈誰が知ろう〉 118 ㊁

50 〈存在のもつ静寂は時に〉 120 ㊃

51 〈親しい風景たちの中でさえ〉 122 ㊅

52 〈私がこの野を歩いている時〉 124 ㊇

53 (影もない曇った昼に) 124

54 (私と同じ生まれのものたちから) 126

55 (無為のうちに) 128

56 (世界は不在の中の
ひとつの小さな星ではないか) 130

57 (私が歌うと) 132

58 (遠さの故に) 134

59 (云い古された言葉を云うだけで) 136

60 (さながら風が木の葉をそよがすように) 138

61 (心は世界にそっと触れる) 140

62 (世界が私を愛してくれるので) 142

㊸ 83
㊺ 85
㊼ 94
㊻ 96
㊽ 97
㊾ 98
㊿ 92
51 95
52 89
53 91

未発表36篇

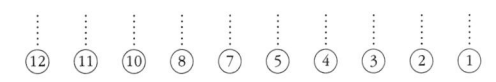

1 朝 148

2 留守 150

3 (なべてのむなしいものよ) 152

4 (歌うことが死を攻める) 154

5 (眠っていた) 156

6 (背負うこと) 158

7 (もしかすると……?) 160

8 今日 162

9 (黙っているすべての前で) 164

10 (むしろ私の幻の中に) 166

⑫ ⑪ ⑩ ⑧ ⑦ ⑤ ④ ③ ② ①

11 夜の業 168
12 忘れ去られて 170
13 (ただ限りなく知られぬことがある) 172
14 高貴な平手打 174
15 口答え 176
16 伴奏 178
17 ふたつの心 180
18 私の旅 182
19 挨拶の必要 184
20 工場 186
21 かつて神が 188
22 ある警句 190

㉙ ㉘ ㉖ ㉕ ㉔ ㉒ ㉑ ⑲ ⑱ ⑯ ⑭ ⑬

雪 192

23 （何気なくうつってゆく午後の陽差の中にいると） 194 ㊳

24 （不幸を知った時に） 196 ㊺

25 （ささやかなひとつの道を歩き続けると） 198 ㊵

26 （同じ陽 同じ空） 200 ㊿

27 （小鳥らは虫を啄む） 202 ㊶

28 （私は華麗な模様の上を） 204 ㊻

29 （はなれていると） 206 ㊌

30 （世界を見廻していると） 208 ㊳

31 （静かな愛のように） 210 ㊳

33 (何かが微笑みのように私の傍を過ぎて行った) 212 ⑧⓪

34 (それは夏のめであった) 214 ⑧①

35 (闇の中で) 218 ⑨⓪

36 (どんな小さな憩いが) 218 ⑨③

あとがき 220

○詩篇の番号について

著者所蔵の自筆ノートに記された詩篇の順番を表す番号を、目次に添えた。例えば、ソネット「9 困却」の下部に「⑳ 孤独」とあるのは、自筆ノートでの順番と、そこに付されたタイトルを表している。

62のソネット＋36

一九五二年春から一九五三年秋

I

1 木蔭

とまれ喜びが今日に住む
若い陽の心のままに
食卓や銃や
神さえも知らぬ間に
木蔭が人の心を帰らせる
今日を抱くつつましさで

ただここへ
人の佇(たたず)むところへと

空を読み
雲を歌い
祈るばかりに喜びを呟く時

私が忘れ
私が限りなく憶えているものを
陽もみつめ　樹もみつめる

2　憧れ

初夏の陽の幸福な宿命の蔭で
私の希(のぞ)みはうとんぜられ
私の憧れだけが駈け廻った
はかなしとふり返る暇もなく
信ずることなく愛してしまった
すべてのゆかしいたたずまいを

それを誰の媚態と云えるだろう
野も雲も愚かなものと知りながら
やがて私の小さな墓のまわりに
人と岩と空とが残る　しかし
いつまでも誰が明日を憶えていよう
私は神をも忘れてしまった
生きないで一体何が始まるのだ
初夏の陽の不思議に若い宿命の蔭で

3 帰郷

ここが異郷だったのだ
わびしい地球の内玄関で
私は奥の暗さにひきこまれた
いろいろな室(へや)の深く隠微なたたずまいに
私が誰か?
帰るすべを知るよしもなく

私は便りを書き続ける
私の限りの滞在について

もはや他の星に憧れず
この星に永遠よりもおもしろく住むことについて
しかしなおいつか帰るとの二伸と共に

おそらく私の予期せぬ帰郷がある
親しい私の異郷からの
私のいない　私の知らない帰郷がある

4 今日

ふたたび日曜日が　そうして
ふたたび月曜日が
ふたたび曇り　ふたたび晴れ
してその先に何がある？

その先など知りはしない
あるのはただ今日ばかり

僕の中にふたたびではなく
今日だけがある

思い出は今日であった
死は今日であるだろうそして
生きることそれが烈(はげ)しく今日である

今日を愛すること
ひとつの短かい歌が死に
今日が小さな喪に捧げられるまで

5　偶感

生きることかくの如きか
朝陽の道を人人は急ぎ
小児ら雀に似て笑い過ぎ
思う者の妄想巷(ちまた)に風のようである

永遠より前に今日が歌う
永遠より若く永遠より難解に

永遠より遠く
永遠よりなお永遠に

街に村に砂漠に海に
おもしろき　おそろしき　かなしき話限りなく
むなしい論にさえ人は日夜眼を輝かせる

思うに生きることかくの如きか
今日この星に隠微なることごと
神を忘れん程に満ちあふれたり

6 朝 1

朝は曇りたり
雲厚く過ぎたる夜を隠せり
かくして今日も始まりぬと
幼ない希みは呟くのだが——
始まるに時なく所なし
私が生き

私が日日を殺してゆく
ただ心のみをあふれさせて

私はあふれる心を信ずる
その無意味な涙を私は信ずる
平安や証しについて何ひとつ知らぬままに

朝は曇
万象未だ夜を残して黙する中に
心あふれたり貧しきものの心あふれたり

7 朝 2

歌っていた 朝の食事を
画いていた 心の飲みものを
何と何とが結ばれているか
大きな調和の予感の中に

朝 光の喜びと目覚めの苦しみと
そして白い衣服をつけて起きた

新たに思い新たに歌おうと
しかしもはや眠らぬ心と共に

死は地から来る　そうして
未来から
今日死に　人は無智に残される

しかしすべてのひろがりに心は応えねばならぬ
此処(ここ)からはるかなことへと
心は常に生き始める

8　笑い

不幸を忘れる程に
不幸ではなかった
幸福を忘れる程に
幸福ではなかった

陽が昼を　そして
星が夜を語り続けた

むしろ大層美しい沈黙が
誰の心でもない私の心を……
今だけを知っている
去(い)くものも来るものも
在ることは流れない
訊ねる心も許されぬ
そんな今を終えることもなく
しかしある日ふと人は笑うだろう

9　困却

人がうじゃうじゃいる
というのが社会である
びしょたれた奴が一匹いる
というのが孤独であるように
困却する
僕はすべてに困却する

神が僕を雇っているのに
政治家も僕を雇おうとする

その他いろいろ
少女や風邪ひきや哲学や
しかも運命はやたらに細かく彫りたがる

だから十四行のつつましやかなうさばらし
聞く人もあるまじ
それ故孤独なりと云う愚者ありやなしや

10　知られぬ者

自動車が云った
鉛筆が云った
化学が云った
お前さんが私をつくったのだ人間よと

狸はそれをどう思ったろう
星はそれをどう思ったろう

神はそれをどう思ったろう
みちあふれた情熱のしかし愚かな傲慢を
さびしいことを忘れた人から
順々に死んでゆけ
知られぬ者ここに消ゆと
風は夕暮の地球に吹き又見知らぬ星に吹いた
神は夕暮の地球を歩き
又見知らぬ星の上を歩いた

11 沈　黙

沈黙が名づけ
しかし心がすべてを迎えてなおも満たぬ時
私は知られぬことを畏れ──
ふとおびえた

失われた声の後にどんな言葉があるだろう
かなしみの先にどんな心が

生きることと死ぬこととの間にどんな健康が
私は神——と呟きかけてそれをやめた
常に私が喋らねばならぬ
私について世界について
無智なるものと知りながら
もはや声なくもはや言葉なく
呟きも歌もしわぶきもなく　しかし
私が——すべてを喋らねばならぬ

12 廃墟

神をもとめる祈りもなく
神を呪う哲学もなく
さながら無のようにかすかに
そこにはただ神自身の歌ばかりがあった
私はもはや歌わぬだろう
たしかな幸福の昨日について

寂寥の予感あふれる明日について
そしてはるかにむなしい快晴の今日について

廃墟は時の骨だ
今日の風が忘れる方へ吹いてゆき
人の意味は晴れわたった空に消える

廃墟はただ佇むことを憧れる
若い太陽の下に
意味もなく佇むためにのみ佇むことを

13 今

輝きは何を照らしてもよい
すべてが私を忘れてくれる
今に棲み
限りなく私が今を愛する時
いつまでも黙っている歌の中に
あまりにかすかな神の気配がして——

それから私がふと今に気付く
ただ静かなひろがりの中で
私が今の豊かさを信ずる時
この星にいて死を知りながら
私は自由だ
情熱は何をみたしてもよい
陽のように空のように
あふれるあまり黙って輝くもの達の下で

14　野にて

私の心が私を去らせた
時を見る高さにまで
私は回想され
神の恣意は覗き見された

歌もなく　意志ももたず
今日私は帰りたがる小学生に似ていた

しかし誰が何を償うことが出来るか
むしろこのような晴れた昼に
人は正しく歌えない
無を語る言葉はなく
すべてを語る言葉もない
しかし私の立つ所にすべてがある
街に人　野に草　そして
天に無

15　鋳型

荒々しく雲は投げられ
山は遠く陽に耐えようとしていた
風景は暮れ
私の心の凹凸そのままに影をひいた
それらは喜びの鋳型であった
陰の方向から喜びを待ち

しかし自ら決して喜びにならない
それらは満たされねばならなかった

喜びを鋳るのは悲しみではない
見知らぬ未完の恣意の中で
私の心は名づけられなかった

満たされそして満たされたものを型どった後で
それらは忘れ去られるであろう
暮れ方の風景と名づけられぬ私の心と

16 朝 3

灯は夜中ともっていた
夜明けに手紙が着いた
空は惚けていた
子等はまだ眠っていた

私は起き上る
私は捨てる

私は拾う
そして忙しくなる

人が歩き始める
私は忘れ始める
神は泣き始める

夜になったら何もかも無くなってしまうだろう
急にそんな予感がする
その時　突然最初の陽が射す

17 始まり

人がいないと私の中に
忘れっぽい夢がいる
時が私を追い越してゆく
私は苦笑する

私は逃げる
とまたもや近づきすぎてしまう

怖しいものの形ばかりにさわっていると
やがて唯ひとつの心に気付く

そしらぬ顔で
私は時を小包にしてしまう
それを送る　昨日の方へ

だが私に捨てることの出来ぬものがある
それらを抱き続けると
俄(にわ)かにもはや新たな始まりだ

18 鏡

心の物音に耳を澄ませていると
私の形がおぼろげになる
私が心を持っている時
それは動かないと弱々しい
私の外にすべてがある
私は外へはいってゆこうとする

しかし外は私を拒む

私の心は疲れてしまう

私の中には考える鏡だけがある
私の鏡はあまりに素直なので
見たものすべてをうつしてしまう
そしてうつったものはもはや在るものではない
私は鏡をみつめながら出ようとする
私の中の私の姿は遠ざかりしかし決して消え去らない

19 ひろがり

ものたちのひろがりの中を
私は歩き続ける
ふと風が立つ
すると時が身動きする
ひそかな身ぶりも
だがすぐ忘れられる

人の気づかぬひろがりの中に
時の死がある

人間の想い及ばぬひろがりに気づいていよう
私に無関心なものたちの間で
生き死ぬことを知ろう

私は歩き続ける　さながら私もものであるかのように
私は見るのをやめる
その時突然私は生き始める

20 心について

私は生きることに親しくなっていった
私は姿ばかりを信じ続けて
心について何ひとつ知らないのだったが
それがかえって私の孤独を明るくした
私はむしろ心に疲れていたのかもしれぬ
もろもろの姿の毅然としたひろがり

それらは心よりもきっぱりと
　時を生き　所を占める

今　私に歌がない
私は星々と同じ生まれだ
私は心をもたぬものの子だ
だがその時突然私に心が還ってくる
私の姿が醜い故に？
いやむしろ世界の姿があまりに美しい故に

21 歌

私が目を挙げた時
もはやその雲の姿はなかった
それらのうつろいやすい姿の中よりもむしろ外に
私に親しい心があった
昔からの祈りが
それらの姿を刻々に呪い続ける

天に何ものも無くそして地に心のある時
雲はそれらの間で常に何ものかになりたがっている
だが何になれるというのだろう？
軽やかにむしろ心に憧れているかのように軽やかに
雲は自らの姿を滅そうとし続ける

地にはすべてがあまりに多く
天にはあまりに少いため
私が歌いたくなるらしい

22 姿について

姿の予感と
姿の悔いとが晴れすぎた空におびただしい
姿自身は
まるで心のように見えないのに
真の姿は心をもたない
うつろいやすいのは姿なのだ

みにくさをおそれ
また滅びをおそれるのも
だが姿を信じ　そして
姿を愛することが喜びだ
むしろ姿の外の心を信じて
今日この晴れすぎた空の下に
心は只ひとつしかなく
あたりには姿ばかりが美しい

23 雲

今朝は雲が大層美しかった
心をもたずしかしさながらひとつの心に照らされているかのように
自らを輝くにまかせたまま
それらはひととき慰めのように流れていった……
私の信じ私の愛することの出来る
さまざまなものがある

それらが私を生かし続け
それらが私に心を与える

はかなさのままに
ひとの心は計り難い
あまりに遠く或はあまりに近く……

だが樹が生き　ひとが生きる
たしかな時と所とをもち続けながら——
今朝私は心に宛てぬ手紙を書く

24 夢

ひとときすべてを明るい嘘のように
私は夢の中で目ざめていた
私は何の証しももたなかった
幸せの思い出の他に

ひとの不在の中にいて
今日　私はすべてを余りに信じすぎる

そうしてふとひそかな不安が私を責める
不幸せさえも自らに許した時に

樹の形　海の形　そして陽……
風景の中のひとを私は想う
そのままに心のようなその姿を

私はかつて目ざめすぎた
今日私は健やかに眠るだろう
夢の重さを証しするために

II

25

世界の中で私が身動きする
すると世界もかすかに身じろぎする
世界がふとふり向くと
天の鳥たちがいっせいに飛び立つ
空が急に空虚になる
書かれた文字は眩しすぎる

私は小手をかざす
すると遠い山山ばかりがはっきりする

天がのさばりだす
私は看病することを知らない
時が疲れる

私は歩いてゆく
世界が私をみつめている
私は死の方へ目をそらす

26

ひとが私に向かって歩いてくる
すれ違いざま私は愛する
だが遠さが速い
忘却がひとを追い越す

街で買うと
孤独がお釣に来る

それを何に費(つか)おうかと
あてどもなく歩き廻る

ふと旗が空で合図する
私は小さな時間を投げてやる
すると夕暮を毀(こわ)してしまう

帰ろうとすると足どりを忘れる
夜が私に媚び始める
だが明日が私をいじめる気配がある

27

地球は火の子供で身重だ
だがおそらく産むことはないらしいので
雲はむしろ死のための綿になりたがる
しかしそれにしては雲は余りに泣きすぎる
時計が時間に不平を云い続ける
時間が飽きると

猫までが欠伸(あくび)する
私は島のようにひとりになる

昼には夜が罪せられ
夜には昼が罪せられる
私はすべてを弁護したい

私が何気なく立上ると
世界が私についてくる
私はつと便所に入る

28

眠ろうとすると
夢が目の中へ入ってしまう
痛みで私の目はさえる
私は哲学の透明度を計る
花も自家用の生を生きている
私は多くの生に触って歩く

私の指はだんだん感じなくなる
最後に死がそれを凍傷にする

私は踊る
すると沢山蹴とばす
世界が玩具の楽器になる

私は疲れる
今度は眠れる
だが夢のない夜の黒さが忘れられない

29

私は思い出をひき写している
古い幻は皆気だてがいい
冬の陽差が私の指に暖かい
今日の空椅子にも陽差がある
窓の外と中との中間に
世界の絵の断片がある

私はそれに触ろうとする
と美しいものは駈け去ってしまう
私はすべてを見つめ続ける
心がいやいや呟いている
愛がそれを黙らせる
今日が帰ってくる
昨日の後姿がもう杳(くら)い
明日の姿は想像出来ない

30

私は言葉を休ませない
時折言葉は自ら恥じ
私の中で死のうとする
その時私は愛している
何も喋らないものたちの間で
人だけが饒舌(じょうぜつ)だ

しかも陽も樹も雲も
自らの美貌に気づきもしない
速い飛行機が人の情熱の形で飛んでゆく
青空は背景のような顔をして
その実何も無い
私は小さく呼んでみる
世界は答えない
私の言葉は小鳥の声と変らない

31

世界の中の用意された椅子に座ると
急に私がいなくなる
私は大声をあげる
すると言葉だけが生き残る
神が天に嘘の絵具をぶちまけた
天の色を真似ようとすると

絵も人も死んでしまう
樹だけが天に向かってたくましい

私は祭の中で証ししようとする
私が歌い続けていると
幸せが私の背丈を計りにくる

私は時間の本を読む
すべてが書いてあるので何も書いてない
私は昨日を質問攻めにする

32

時折時間がたゆたいの演技をする
そのすきに私は永遠の断片を貯めこむ
私は自分の生の長さを計る
私は未知のことを予感する

風が立つ
思い出から私は未来を設計する

陽が高い
夏をくり返そうとする私の決意！

かくして私の中に積まれてゆく
雑多な悔い　雑多な予感がある
それらが古びる時に私は死に親しい

だが今日まだ私は若さの頭痛に悩まされる
陣痛のようにそれは産みたがる
私は駈け出す　私は浪費せねばならぬ

33

私は近づこうとした
すると私はふたたび遠ざかった
私は遠ざかろうとした
すると私はふたたび近づいた
自らを絶えず忘れ果てながら
心は見事な身ぶりをする

私は心の秩序を見ようとして
人の森で迷子になった

だが私は常に生きる喜びを云いわけにもつ
私の愛は跳ねている
時折すべてに無関心な程に

青空は屋根ではなく古井戸だ
私は身投げする
私は生きかえってしまう

34

風のおかげで樹も動く喜びを知っている
太陽は産婆ぶっているので
若いくせにえらがっている
私は太陽を嗅いでみる
音楽が終る
私に生の重みが滲み透る

私がうつむくと
ふと幸せが私の顔をのぞきこむ

私は生に用事がないので
いつも歌ってばかりいる
だが私は頌(ほ)めることを知っている

空の青いところへたどり着くと
きっと誰もいない
あれは恵み深い嘘なのだ

35

街から帰ってくると
私の室にそしらぬ顔で静けさがいる
私が黙って窓を開けると
黒い絵の流れこむ気配がする
灯が夜をみつめていると
夜の呟きがあからさまになる

私の中に季節の絵がある
生きられていないのでそれらは贅沢に美しい

遠くから声がする
誰を呼んでいるのでもない
只空へ向かって捨てられている

昼の瞳孔がまだひろがらない
闇の中の姿は見分け難く
星の数だけが限りない

36

私があまりに光をみつめたので
私の影は夜のように暗かった
私はさびしさを計算する
しかしそれには解がない
ふたたびあらゆる遠さが私に帰ってくる
私は私とだけ親しい

私の言葉は捨て所がない
私はそれを汗に変えようと企む

天は変らぬ退屈な大道具だ
すべてがその下にあるので
遠さも天で計られる

しかし私が感傷を着ようとすると
不幸なことに袖が短かい
私は幼ない頃を思い出す

37

私は私の中へ帰ってゆく
誰もいない
何処から来たのか？
私の生まれは限りない
私は光のように遍在したい
だがそれは不遜なねがいなのだ

私の愛はいつも歌のように捨てられる
小さな風になることさえかなわずに
生き続けていると
やがて愛に気づく
郷愁のように送り所のない愛に……
人はそれを費ってしまわねばならない
歌にして　汗にして
あるいはもっと違った形の愛にして

38

私が生きたら
物語が終らなくなってしまった
いつまでも忘れないと
老いた神々が眠れない
ささやかな言葉が
夜の中で囁き交わされる

昼の歌が凍っている
囁きたちはその上をすべってゆく

鋭くしじまの中にうかぶ
かえって生の姿が
不吉な鳥が叫ぶと

物語る人は私だ
私の訥弁(とつべん)を風が運ぶ
大分離れてから「愛が……」などときこえている

39

雲はあふれて自分を捨てる
何故それが雨なのか?
人はあふれて心を捨てる
何故それが歌なのか?
気弱なものたちが
世界の名を呼び続ける

だが樹は答えない
樹は自ら世界となるのに忙しい
自分があるひろがりの部分だと気づくと
人は俄かに強がりを云う
私は樹よりもえらいのだなどと
だから樹もきこえないように呟いている
大事なのは歌ではなくて
むしろ心を捨てることだと

40

遠さのたどり着く所を空想していると
私に近いものたちが呟き出す
愛は気まぐれな散歩者だから
いつも汗ばんで戻ってくる
さびしい方へ駈け出して
やがて餓えたように帰ってきても

もはやにぎやかなところが見つからない
昔からのしきたりで夜は独りの愛に冷たい
不在の交代のように
昼があり　夜がある
愛もそこへは駈けこめない
私が去ってしまうと
残された夜が美しい
私を惜しむ気配もなく……

空の青さをみつめていると
私に帰るところがあるような気がする
だが雲を通ってきた明るさは
もはや空へは帰ってゆかない
陽は絶えず豪華に捨てている
夜になっても私達は拾うのに忙しい

人はすべていやしい生まれなので
樹のように豊かに休むことがない

窓があふれたものを切りとっている
私は宇宙以外の部屋を欲しない
そのため私は人と不和になる

在ることは空間や時間を傷つけることだ
そして痛みがむしろ私を責める
私が去ると私の健康が戻ってくるだろう

空を陽にすかしていると
無のもつ色が美しい
時が私に優しく訊ねるが
私は黙っている

昨日の朝を私に返せ
失われてしまった風景のために

私は何をしてやることも出来ない
ただ弔うことのほかに

今日　期待は明日に似ている
だが明日になると
期待は今日にすぎない

しかし私のまわりに晴天の一日がある
子供の時から私は何が好きで生きてきたか？
ふと私に近く何かのよみがえる気配がする

43

あふれた空の光を
雲がそこここであつめていた
風が耳打ちすると
ふと大きな不在が目をさます

ふり向くと人がいる
私は言葉をそっと置き去りにする

人がそれらに礼儀正しい
私は椅子のように世界に腰かける

地の物音を
人人が拾い集める
だが私を納得させるどんなひそかな呟きもない

むしろ私を知らぬものたちの間で
私は時折風のような幸せに気づく
その時私は帰ってきている

私は闘士であったから
青空を盾にもち
夜の中をしのび足だ
私は世界からさらに遠くを目指したのだが……
あてどないさまよいの眼(まなこ)して
私は敵のない戦いを続けている

暗い中に世界のしわぶきの気配がする
私はきっとなる

だが私の中の知られぬものと
私の外の知られぬものと
それらのつながりの上で私は眩暈(めまい)してしまう

その時私の血が遠くひいてゆく
私は昏(くら)い思い出にしばられる
私はもはや勇ましくない

45

風が強いと
地球は誰かの凧のようだ
昼がまだ真盛りの間から
人は夜がもうそこにいるのに気づいている
風は言葉をもたないので
ただいらいらと走りまわる

私は他処(よそ)の星の風を想う
かれらはお互いに友達になれるかどうかと
地球に夜があり昼がある
そのあいだに他の星たちは何をしているのだろう
黙ってひろがっていることにどんな仕方で堪えているのか？
昼には青空が嘘をつく
夜がほんとうのことを呟く間私たちは眠っている
朝になるとみんな夢をみたという

若い陽がひととき
夜につながる私の内部を明るくする
光の中に埃が夥(おびただ)しい
それらは病の前兆ではないのか
私の足がいつ地から奪ったことがあるか
樹々のたくましい根のように

昼を頌める前にいつ私が空を抱いたか
若い枝々がしているように

ひそかな子守唄さえあきらめて
せめて私はもの達の眠りを妨げぬようにしよう
夜を知るのは愚かなことだ……
夜にはみんな黙っていなければならない
星たちに問いかけてはならない
あれらは冷い笑いさえもっていない

111

47

時が曇った夜空に滲みてゆく
私が動くと時が雪のようにちりかかる
私の心は寒がっている
私の血だけが暖かい

昼間楽しかったものが息をひそめると
もう駈け廻っても見つからない

私の頭に空想の年月がある
私はそれに火をつける

思い出が燃え
予感が燃えると
今日がしらじらと焼け残る

本当にあることが信じられない
そこで夢とひきかえに明日を貰う
目を覚ますと朝食の香が馨しい

私たちはしばしば生の影が
しめやかな言葉で語られるのを聞く
墓　霊柩車　遺言などと
けれどもそれらは死について何も云いはしない
生きている私たちは影よりも遠くを知らない
無を失うことを私たちは知らない

私たちは鏡をもちすぎている
そのためいつもうつされた生ばかりを覗いている
やがて鏡もない死の中で
私たちは自らに気づかずにすむだろう
私たちは世界と一体になれるだろう……
しかし今日雨の街に生者たちは生きるのに忙しい
夕刊には自殺者の記事がある
私たちは死をとりかこむ遠さにすぎない

III

49

誰が知ろう
愛の中の私の死を
むしろ欲望をそのやさしさのままに育てよう
ふたたび世界の愛をうばうために
ひとをみつめる時に
生の姿が私を世界の中へ帰らせる

若い樹とひとの姿とが
時折私の中で同じものになる

心を名づけることもなしに
ひとの噤(つぐ)んだ口に触れて私の知ることを
大きな沈黙がさらってゆく

しかしその時私もその沈黙なのだ
そして私も樹のように
世界の愛をうばっている

50

存在のもつ静寂は時に
無のもつそれにもましてかすかだ
だが近づくと
かれらのひそかな身ぶりがあらわになる
かれらは訴えてはいないだろうか
一本の樹　ひとつの椀

ひとりの娘　一枚の絵
と呼ばれることの不安について

在ることのたしかさについて
私もよく知っている　しかし
人のそとに名づけられる何があるか

無こそむしろ安易なものだ
私が呼んでも世界は目ざめない
私は愚かに愛することが出来るだけだ

51

親しい風景たちの中でさえ
世界の豊かさは難解だ
久しいものの行方よりも
今あるすべてを私は知りたい
やがて亡びるものたちのひたむきな姿が
私を簡素な想いに誘う

親しい今の中でだけ
私の想いは死に阻まれない

だが空と陽のしじまの中で
奪われ続ける今の痛みが
ふと私を怖れさせる

しかし世界の中へ私は帰る
別れのない日が一日とてあったろうか
そのような世界の中へ私は帰る

52

私がこの野を歩いている時
あの森にはどんな風が吹いているのか
空があのやさしい狭さで
無を後手にかくしているうちに
私が帰りかけている時に
いつも私から逃げてゆくものがある

私は私の不在にとりかこまれている
それを支えるため私は疲れる

だがひととき陽はすべてを無分別に照らし出す
あまりにあらわな風景の中で
私の影は夜よりも黒い

その時私の不在は樹や雲やひとびとによって満たされている
私の愛がそれらを証しする
私はむしろ私の不在にもたれ始める

影もない曇った昼に
私は言葉の病んでゆくのを見守っていた
むしろ樹や草たちに私の歌はうたわれ
憧れはいつも地に還った

始め不気味な沈黙から
私たちは突然饒舌の世界にとびこんでしまう

言葉は人の間で答をもつかし
人のそとで言葉はいつも病んでゆく

すべてがそこから生まれてきた始めの沈黙の中に
なお健やかな言葉を
私も樹や草のようにもちたいのだが——
どんな言葉が私に親しいのか
むしろ私が歌うことなく
私の歌われるのを私は聞く……

54

私と同じ生まれのものたちから
私はいつか離れすぎた
地のものたちの間に
もはや私は帰ってゆけない
だが愛でさえ己れのものにすぎぬと気づく時
誰が祈らずにいられよう

すべてが生き続けてゆくようにと
その祈りの貧しさにむしろ心安らかに
私は何を持つことも出来ない
たとえ私が愛していても
樹や雲やひとを
私はただ捨てることが出来るだけだ
あふれる私の心を
それを愛と呼ぶことさえためらいがちに

55

無為のうちに
私は私の生を実らせる
樹が佇み続けることで
生きることの大きなめぐりに与(あずか)っているように
私に許された日日を
ただ誠実に遊ぶため

私は佇み続ける
やがて心を失うまで

私は捨てられた皿だ
満たされぬことを知りながら
なお待つ形のまま……

そしてもし世界の中で
私も役目をもっているとしたら
そのように佇むことが私に課せられている

56

世界は不在の中のひとつの小さな星ではないか
夕暮……
世界は所在なげに佇んでいる
まるで自らを恥じているとでもいうように
そのようなひととき
私は小さな名ばかりを拾い集める

そしていつか
私は口数少なになる

時折物音が世界を呼ぶ
私の歌よりももっとたしかに
遠い汽笛　犬の吠声　雨戸のまた刻みものの音……
その時世界は夕闇のようにひそかに
それらにききいっている
ひとつひとつの音に自らをたしかめようとするかのように

57

私が歌うと
世界は歌の中で傷つく
私は世界を歌わせようと試みる
だが世界は黙っている
言葉たちは
いつも哀れな迷子なのだ

とんぼのようにかれらはものの上にとまっていて
夥しい沈黙にかこまれながらふるえている
かれらはものの中に逃げようとする
だが言葉たちは
世界を愛することが出来ない
かれらは私を呪いながら
星空に奪われて死んでしまう
――私はかれらの骸(むくろ)を売る

遠さの故に
山は山になることが出来る
近く見つめすぎると
山は私に似てしまう
広い風景は人を立止まらせる
その時人は自らをかこむ夥しい遠さに気づく

それらはいつも
人を人にしている遠さなのだ

だが人は自らの中に
ひとつの遠さをもつ
そのため人は憧れつづける……

いつか人はあらゆる遠さに犯された場所にすぎぬ
もはや見られることもなく
その時人は風景になる

云い古された言葉を云うだけで
むしろ言葉もなく
動かされる心をもっているだけで
私は満ち足りた

雨が降ってきた
女の子が走ってくる

あ　風だ……と
それらがもはや私のうた

いく度も飽きることなく
私は世界の名を呼ぶ
私の愛するものたちの名を

そして不幸せさえも
私が頌め続けているうちに
時折私も名付親になることが出来る

さながら風が木の葉をそよがすように
世界が私の心を波立たせる
時に悲しみと云い時に喜びと云いながらも
私の心は正しく名づけられない
休みなく動きながら世界はひろがっている
私はいつも世界に追いつけず

夕暮や雨や巻雲の中に
自らの心を探し続ける

だが時折私も世界に叶う
風に陽差に四季のめぐりに
私は身をゆだねる──

──私は世界になる
そして愛のために歌を失う
だが　私は悔いない

心は世界にそっと触れる
その形のままに心はうなずき続ける
いま風が立った……
いま少年が駈けてゆく……と
心はまた自らに触れる　そして
世界と分つことの出来ない己れの中へ

心はいつも帰ってゆく
ためらいながらもうたうために——

私の頌めうたを誰が拾う?
喜びはむしろ地に帰るのがふさわしい
その時喜びは孤(ひと)りの中で朽ち果てない
黙ったままでいいのだ
愛を——
世界は私の眼差だけで気づいているだろう

62

世界が私を愛してくれるので
(むごい仕方でまた時に
やさしい仕方で)
私はいつまでも孤りでいられる

私に始めてひとりのひとが与えられた時にも
私はただ世界の物音ばかりを聴いていた

私には単純な悲しみと喜びだけが明らかだ
私はいつも世界のものだから

空に樹にひとに
私は自らを投げかける
やがて世界の豊かさそのものとなるために

……私はひとを呼ぶ
すると世界がふり向く
そして私がいなくなる

未発表36篇

1　朝

ふたたび青空は始まっていた
僕の上に　そしてすべての人人の上に
光は朝来る
またはじめてのことのために
希望も慰めも安心もなく
生きることはしかしひろがっていた

知っていることは何もなかったが
喜びとすべてを呼ぶことが出来た

何の知恵もなく死はやって来た
それが奇怪なこととは思われなかった
墓のかたちさえ空しい意味に満ちあふれ……
ふたたびすべては始まっていた
終ることを苦しみながら
証しも意味もなくただ始まることのために

2　留　守

私の心を支えてくれる
歌と空とそうして
今日　冬陽の中の私の留守
私のいない幸福の椅子
光もない暗い宇宙に坐っていた
自分の涙を百貨店で買って飲んだ

苦さと名づける知恵もなしに
ただむなしいことのために

今日もひねもす忘れていた
忘れているのを知りながら
小さな神や悪魔の雑踏の中に

明日もひねもす……
しかし失われぬという証しもなく
賢く人は忘れようとする

3

なべてのむなしいものよ
僕を支えてあれ
歌よ　空よ　今日よ
お前達の心も語らずにただ
喜びも悲しみも涙から生れる
僕の前に泣いているものはないが

笑いも怒りも失われる

山山がそして空がみつめる時

眼をはいってゆくと出られない
心がいつまでも呟いている夜と
心がいつまでも歌っている昼と

星の上に誰が住む？
すべての顔を見ながら
心について何ひとつ知らずに？

4

歌うことが死を攻める
満ちそしてあふれることが昼ある
そうしてしかし　いつまでももどかしい心を
揺籠はもう昔にふりおとしてしまった

日日を飢えて
心には傷もなく　　だが

あまりに素直にすぎる心は
故里をもたない　罰せられて
神に罰せられた心は
神に賞(め)でられたことから
はばたかず空を知り
平穏をもはや忘れ
幸福や不幸の呼名を忘れた
ただ生きることだけを覚えるために

5

眠っていた
いったい何時の夜を？
いったい何時の昼を？
見知らぬ夢に迷いながら

来ることか　行くことか　それとも
はるかに帰ることか

歩みもせずに夢みていた
うらやましい幼児の心で

だが知らねばならぬ
光が生まれ　光が死に
泣く暇もない程に

墓までを歩み　そうして
何に気付くのだろう？
陽とはてもない空の昼に

6

背負うこと
それが正しい宿命だ
火花や唸りもなく
ひとときひとときを充たしてゆくそれが
暗い宇宙をそのように
ひとり動いて充たしてゆき

やがて明るい牧場をと
しかしさびしい百年の間に

百年ではなかったのだ
今日をと
心は悟るのだが

やがて消え
やがて失われること
それがはるかに残ることなのだと

7

もしかすると……?
では一体愚かなこととはどんなことだ
光が生き　光が死に
樹はそれらすべてを黙っている

堪えることとも云わず
あるものをすべてその通りに

それだけがあるのだと感ずるままに
静かな知恵に

樹はむしろ深く湛えている
原生の昔から
誰のためにでもなく
あることをそのままに賢く
自分の知らぬことを
生きているままに

8 今 日

償われた――
ひそかな雪の夜に
むなしいものの上に白く
白くただ知られぬ美しさに

烈しく老い
地をもたず

時の池に沈んだ重い夢よ
お前の恐ろしさも

さあれ終りはしない
夏に希み
秋に悔いながら

今日をそうしてふたたび今日を
さながら冷い時そのままに
さながら冷い所そのままに

9

黙っているすべての前で
心だけが聞こうとあせっていた
顔だけのすべての前で
心だけが仲間を探していた
誰かがたしかにうたっている
自分のいじらしい幻のほかに

しかし心はむしろ
自らの微笑をつくった

あきらめねばならぬ百年の間に
しかし決してあきらめることなく
死をさえも知りながら死ぬだろうと

答えないすべての前で
心はむしろ
自らをうたった

10

むしろ私の幻の中に
私は自分の心を探した
日は数々の問を暮れ
夜は黙って名付親を待っていた
　誰が問い　誰が名づけ
　誰が自分の心を重いと云うのか

黙っているものは強かった
何も知らぬものは強かった　しかし

私は知っている
ひとつの心を　そして
そのような今日の重さを
名づけられるものがもはや死に
知りながら私が黙る時
心は失われるだろう

11 夜の業(わざ)

祝は空に　そして
喪は地に　と人は云う
では呪うのは誰か
あのすばやい夜の業で
走り打つ昼は眠り
思う昼は眠らない

病が見　そして
夜が目覚めてしまう

陽は星の意味を云い
星は陽の心を云った
私は聞いていた　疎みながら

それから空は沈黙した
問い　病む前に捧げること
ひとつの心こそすべての心と知りながら

12 忘れ去られて

かくあることはやがて
かくてあったと語られ
しかしかくてあったことは
かくあることの中でしか生きない

幸福とひとりは云い
不幸とひとりは云った

して何を？
知らぬ愚かさを悔いるすべもなく

ふたたびくり返そうとする手に心に
葉は落ち　白く正しい雪は降る
しかしもはや思い出の中にではなく

人が生き　そして限りない今の後に
時さえも天に住むだろう
しかしもはや忘れ去られて

13

ただ限りなく知られぬことがある
野に　街に　僕の中に──そうしてしかし
僕は動かねばならぬ
心を泣かせぬために
常に生き終え
生き始めながら

心を負い
心を激しくあきらめようと

心を腕に　涙を汗に
昨日を去らしめ　明日を去らしめ
僕はひとり動かねばならぬ

知られぬ奇怪な地に空に
乾いた意志を捨てながら
突然に今日が暗い記憶となるまで

14 高貴な平手打

去るものの背は
夢の中でもどかしい
祈ることを知っていればと
真昼に悔いる馬鹿もいる
誰が残り
誰が消えて行っちまうか

星から星への輪廻を工夫し
多忙な神が失敗する

誰が一番早く泳ぐか！
阿修羅の如き太鼓打ち！
三行に十年かかる大詩人！

今日にだけ通用する
阿呆らしい情熱の高貴な平手打を
臆病なわるもの共は待ち続ける

15　口答え

もはや僕はおとなになった
とりすました僕の中で
希望は育っちまった僕に似て
おずおず詩など書き始めた
もはや僕はおとなになった
もう貰えるものもない

もはや僕は感じてしまった
生きることをそのいんちきを

されど善良な神は云う
生きてみろよいいもんだぜ
なれなれしげに肩をたたく

僕はもう大きいのだから口答えする
鎮魂行の貸切電車くらい用意しろと
そうでなければすべてを僕に任せてくれと

16 伴奏

人は歌う
何を？　永遠に不思議な何かをだ
そのように突撃喇叭(らっぱ)の哀調も
人の気づかぬ遠い想いをうたっている
あわれに愚かな勇ましさよ
まるで生真面目な遊びのように

伴奏されたむなしい勇気に
火星かどこかの人も顔をしかめる

単細胞から猿経由で
われわれは一体何時不思議な何かに気付いたか
銀河や星雲の冷い横顔！

親しい地球の他に何があるか
親しい今日の他に何があるか
しかもなお伴奏つきで戦争する！

17 ふたつの心

深夜にうたう
蛙の声がある
深夜に鳴り響く
サイレンの音がある

ふたつの心は
もうそれだけで難解すぎる

より強く棲むわれらの心に
だが何かがさびしく訴える

はたして人が理解したのか
それともすべてが最初に在ったのか
畏れなく使い減らすわれらの罪

深夜僕は別に神の手先に会わなかったが
どうやら僕が神の手先のようだ
そしたら人は裏切者と呼ぶだろうか

18　私の旅

私に近い物語
私に遠い物語がある
生きることを予言して
また帰ってくる音楽の中で
はるかな風物に心ひかれ
私の旅は心をめぐる

若い神秘は住まわれてしまい……
しかし新たな地球の上に

星を俯瞰(ふかん)し
そしてふたたび大地の上に住まうこと
夏　空　太陽の答を信じて

ひとりの人にひとつの物語
やがて誰かがそれを歌う
すべて無い安心の地の下に

19 挨拶の必要

私の物差は大きい
二十億光年よりもっと遠く
私の問が反響する
うつろな百年の夜毎に
私は果して人間か
星雲と真空の中にぶらりと

仕方なく意味を遊びながら
私は朝飯を食うのである

大きな不幸の中に
小さな幸福が棲む
もはや心をもて余して

されば街に出(い)で挨拶しよう
私は果して人間かと
地を踏み　陽の心をたしかめるために

20　工　場

誰かが造ってゆくと
みんなが使った
それは高貴な流れ作業だった
怪我については詳らかでないが
草は緑を使った
人は愛を使った

空は憧れを使った
そして私が──心を使った

浪費也　百年の
いや情熱だ　焼きつくす
誰が苦情の責を負うか
やがて工場は破産して
もっと簡単な藻などを造った
年月さえも老いて行った

21 かつて神が

かつて神がいたことを
真空はかすかに記憶していた
昔神が私を創ったと
あるやらないやらの声で呟いた
楽しく落着いた朝の食事
それは神の惰性であるか

誰もいず　何もない
それがひとつの法則なのか

死の後に残るものの冷さよ
他人の眼　砂漠の面　そして
私のいない日月星辰

何処まで何時まで歩けるか？
神の焚火のくすぼりを踏んでから
新しい燐寸(マッチ)を計算しようなどと

22 ある警句

星々は暗夜に落葉し
子供が朝に秋を知る
博士達は眼を伏せて
はかなきことを計算する
例えば石に誰がいるか
神かそれとも細菌か

四季が飽きずに呟き続け
人はしまったとばかり死んでゆく

ある時豪華な地平は開き
たしかに立派な真理は光ると
多くのかなしいお伽話が少年少女をたぶらかしたが

もはや神がひとつの警句である
焦燥の手垢にまみれ
神は日日に使い古される

23 雪

深い雪の高原に
道の意味がある
空までの道の意味が
老いた樹のみる夢に似て
今日をして
空を荷わしめよ

昨日の足跡が

明日の道を忘れる程にも

今日　白く深い雪の中に爪立ちして

悲しみと共に雲を摑もうとするのは誰か

歌いながら尾根を行き

やがて人人の新しい春が雪を消し

ひとつの平凡な凍死体が発見される時

ひとりにとって真実だった道の意味は気付かれない

24

何気なくうつってゆく午後の陽差の中にいると
ふと生きることが肌寒い
何ごとも起らない無為の中に身を置くと
生きることの姿がかえって静かに明るい
すべての故郷(ふるさと)を失ってしまう時があるものだ
山の向こう雲の向こう人のあいだを探しあぐねて

ふたたび人が自分に帰ってくる時
そして自らを故郷と呼ぶにあまりに人が貧しい時……
人はもはや帰るという言葉をあきらめる
ただ生きること
ただここにそして今　生きること——
冬の陽差が私に教える
だが私は若い
私はなおあきらめよりも美しい何ものかを信じ続ける……

25

不幸を知った時に
人は始めて幸福に気付くものだ
だが私はむしろ幸福を知り過ぎている故に
常に不幸に気付いていた
さびしい夜たちだ
星と星との間に眠っている

さびしい昼たちだ
影をなくそうといつも空しく輝いている

そうして　さびしい生たちだ
幸福も不幸も覚束ない
小さな日日を数えている……

気付かぬ人人だけが幸福だ——
幸福に気付き不幸に気付いてしまった時
さびしい怠惰が私のものになる

26

ささやかなひとつの道を歩き続けると
やがて挨拶の出来る親しいものが増えてゆく
小さな歌をうたっていると
うたっている間の幸せが私のものだ
生きていると
死だけがまことの不幸せの名に価する

傷つくことさえ若い私にむしろ快い
痛みが私の生を証しする時に

私にとってかけがえのない一日一日
それらがいつまでも目覚めているといい
ひそやかな　だが確かなひろがりで

やがて私の死の時に
それらの日日こそが私の墓なのだ
私の信ずることの出来た重さのままに

27

同じ陽　同じ空
それらが思い出を信じられるものにする
生きられた日日が
私の中に残しているこのひそやかなひろがりを……
かずかずのものが
その日の幸せの姿をして

私がふり向くのを待っている
その時今日を忘れる罪もおそれずに

私の中をなつかしい姿が過ぎてゆく
その簡素な風景に
死んでしまった遠さがある

やがてまた今日が古い幻になる
だがその度に
私の中に積まれてゆくものがある

28

小鳥らは虫を啄(ついば)む
楽しそうに
小鳥らの上に青空がある
楽しそうに
私も小さな幸せをかくしている
私の不幸がやっかむからだ

私は石を蹴る
するとひとつの星の凹凸が心にうかぶ
やがて愛らしい未来に
私は幾何(いくばく)かを賭ける
敗けた時には賭を忘れている
だがこの無表情な胴元は誰なのだ？
幸せを支配するものに
私は小鳥らを投げつけてやろう

29

私は華麗な模様の上を
とび歩いている
だが時折私もけつまずく
すると模様が居直っている
在るものには尊敬を余儀なくされる
私は腰を低うして

神の作品の展覧を拝見した
私はいくつかを買ってもみた
すべては無料に近い値段である
私の出生さえ安価なものだ
真の価値はただで買える
最後に自分を支払えばよいのだ
だがそこへ行くまでに肥っておくことが肝心だ
私がいたということをはっきりさせておくために

30

はなれていると
ひとは私の知らないところを歩いている
あまりにみつめすぎると
急に私もひとりいなくなってしまう
孤独の中を歩き廻られると
私はかえってひとりになる

ひとがひとりで歩いている時
私は世界の中のひとを愛する

ふと眼が合うと
私たちはお互いを思い出す
その時世界は夢になる

だがひとはみつめない
私は絶えずおそれている
それ故私もみつめない

31

世界を見廻していると
ふとひとの後姿が目に入る
私は自分がひとに向かって
逃げるのを阻もうとする
私の知っているひとも
私にとって見知らぬひとだ

だが私の知っている指に触れると
俄かになつかしくなる

ひとの知っているひろがりがある
風が吹く
私の知っているひろがりがある

ひとが自身をふと覗きこむ時
私はひとの指の冷たさに気づく
突然私は愛し始める

32

静かな愛のように
さりげなく来
さりげなく去ってゆくものが
いつも私の心をひく

生きることもまたそのようなものだろうか
どこから来

どこへ去ってゆくかも知らぬままに
束の間の幸せの姿して……
地の幸せを私は信じる
烈しいものを　そして
つつましいものを　なお
私は樹に似る
黙って――
私は地から享け続ける

33

何かが微笑みのように私の傍を過ぎて行った
しかしそれも去年のことだったのだろうか
私の部屋からいつか優しい人人は去り
今はそこに小さいしかし生意気な時と所ばかりがある
苦笑は壁の形のままにはめられ
私の心は何気ないように窓の外を眺めている

しかし私の部屋に私は住み
青空は苦しいまでに変らない
だがそれもこれも去年のことだったのだろうか
何かしら今は忘れられやすく
私はいつも昨夜に似た今夜ばかりをもってしまう
そう例えば私はこう云うだろう
絶え間なく時が私の今を奪うと
昨夜はもはや私の夜ではないと

1952. 7

34

それは夏の初めであった
絶え間なく終りながら
私を傷つけ しかし
痛々しい程に真実だった

小さな別れと呼ぶことは出来ない
生真面目な少年のように

いつも真実の時が私をみつめる
私に悔いをすすめようと

束の間の喜びで何故満足出来なかったか
空と風と葉のそよぎと　そして
憧れやまぬ私の心と

しかしそれは夏の初めであった
私が時を悔い
私が私の外に心をもとめたのは

1952. 7

闇の中で
記憶だけが私に残される時
暗い花々にかこまれて
私は思い出に捧げられた墓石のようだ
かつてあんなにいきいきと動き廻っていたものが
いまは頑な古さの中に閉じこめられている

僅かな言葉で云い尽くされ
もはや触れることの出来ぬ不確かさで

何気なく生き捨てたかずかずの小さなことが
どんなに貴いことだったか……
もう誰も憶えていない

陽が今日をむごい明るさに照らし出す
しかし記憶はもはや覚めない薄明だ
罪のようにそれは帰るところがない

36

どんな小さな憩いが
私のためにあるのだろう
——やがて
悲しみも喜びも忘れてしまった時に
ただ大きなひろがりについてのかすかな思い出が
まるで悔いられた予感のように私に巣食っている

見知らぬ夢の中で私はひとつひとつ親しいものを数える
しかしそれらを集め終った時に私はすべてを忘れている
私はあのひねもす墓石を磨く墓造りのようだ
彼はひとつの生の小さなかたみを磨き続ける
刻々に輝く墓石に彼は絶えず自らの姿を覗く
だがそこにはどんな証しもない
むしろ絶えず働き続けていることで
彼はわずかに救われている

あとがき

ここに収めた九十八篇の詩はすべて同じ形で書かれていて、それを私は欧米の詩形に倣ってソネットと呼んだ。書いたのは一九五二年四月から一九五三年八月までの間で、そのうちの六十二篇を択んだものが、一九五三年十二月に『62のソネット』という題名で東京創元社から出版され、その後二〇〇一年三月に未刊のもの一篇を加えて、講談社から+α文庫の一冊として出版されたから、今回の出版は三度目ということになる。

二十代の始めに書いたものが、半世紀をへて今も読み継がれているのは、作者にとって嬉しいことであると同時に、不思議なことのようにも感じられる。もしかすると作者の私が気づいていない良さが、これらの詩にはあるのかもしれないと思って、今回は九十八篇すべてを英訳とともに出してもらうことにした。

一九五七年に書いたエッセーで私は「〈六十二のソネット〉は私の青春の書である。私が典型的な若者であり、かつ自らの若さに忠実であったという自負が私

にはある。(中略)それは大ざっぱにいえば、ひとつの生命的なほめうたである。」と書いている。いま思い返してみてもそれはその通りだが、今回の訳者のひとりであり英詩に詳しい川村和夫さんが、訳すのは大変だがそれが楽しいと言ってくださっているのを聞くと、これらのソネット群を成立させている言語が、意識の表層よりもその深層から生まれていることで、語と語の関係にある種の音楽性を獲得していることも魅力のひとつかと思う。

　言い換えると、それは言語としては多義的で曖昧にかたむき、読者にとっては難解だということになる。だが詩は左脳で理解だけすればいいものではなく、右脳の言語化の難しい働きが詩を味わうには不可欠だ。含意が異なる日本語と英語を比較しながら読むことで、また詩の味わい方も違ってくるかもしれない。いずれにせよ、作者は五十数年前の青春と二十一世紀の青春との間に、大きなへだたりがないことを願っている。

二〇〇九年六月

谷川俊太郎

○本書について

 『62のソネット』は一九五三年十二月東京創元社発行の初版を底本に、著者所蔵の自筆ノートを参照して改訂を施した。また、同ノートから、初版発表時に収録されなかった三十六篇のソネットを「未発表36篇」として初めて収録した。「未発表36篇」の収録の順序は、自筆ノートに記された順番に従った。自筆ノートには、最初のページに「一九五二年四月／一九五三年八月」という日付があり、全部で九十八篇のソネットが清書されている。各詩篇には番号が付されており、タイトルの付いているものもある。
 英訳は一九九二年九月、Katydid Books 社発行のW・I・エリオット、川村和夫訳 *62 Sonnets & Definitions* を底本に、新たな改訂を施した。また、「未発表36篇」は「36 Unpublished Sonnets」として、両訳者による新訳を収録した。

〇 校訂について

旧仮名遣いを新仮名遣いに、ひらがなの拗促音は小文字にし、誤植や一字空きの有無、また以後の刊本との異同は、自筆ノートを参照して著者了解のもとに訂正した。

底本のルビ（振り仮名）は生かし、難読と思われる漢字には著者の校閲を得て新たにルビを加えた。常用漢字・人名漢字の旧字体は新字体にあらため、その他は原則として正字体とした。送り仮名は原則として底本通りとした。

英訳には、新たな改訂を施し、日本語底本の訂正などの変更箇所も反映した。また新しい「Preface」を付した。

62 Sonnets + 36

Shuntaro Tanikawa

Translated by
William I. Elliott and Kazuo Kawamura

Shueisha Bunko

62 Sonnets + 36

Shuntaro Tanikawa

Translated by William I. Elliott and Kazuo Kawamura

Book Design / Ariyama design store

First Edition 2009

All rights reserved. No Part of this publication may be reproduced or transmitted in any form or by any means, without permission in writing from the publisher.

Copyright © 2009 Shuntaro Tanikawa, W. I. Elliott, Kazuo Kawamura
ISBN 978-4-08-746459-7

Preface

The sonnet found its earliest major exponent in Francesco Petrarca, who sang over 500 years ago. Although little is known of the object of Petrarca's affections, we can surmise that Laura was elated by such passionate 'little songs.' These were songs in her praise and a passionate confession of his love for her.

When Shuntaro Tanikawa was writing his sonnets in 1952 the "object" of his affection was not a person but life itself. Taken as a whole, Tanikawa's work, too, turns out to be a passionate confession; but if Petrarca celebrated platonic love, Shuntaro hymned his zest for life. His

youthful certainties and uncertainties rest upon the basic assumption that life in all its variegation is good and this assumption has held fast nearly sixty years. Just about everything that characterizes all his subsequent poetry can be found explicitly or implicitly in these two seminal volumes of his verse: *Two-Billion Light-Years of Solitude* and *62 Sonnets*. For devotees of his poetry they are essential reading.

William I. Elliott
Kazuo Kawamura

Contents

Preface 4

I

1 Shadows of Trees 16   ......⑰
2 Longings 17   ......㉗ Forgetting God
3 Homecoming 18   ......㉛
4 Today 19   ......⑮
5 Incidental Thoughts 20   ......㉚
6 Morning (1) 21   ......㉝
7 Morning (2) 22   ......⑥
8 Laughing 23   ......⑨
9 Bewilderment 24   ......⑳ Loneliness
10 The Unknown 25   ......㉓
11 Silence 26   ......㉜
12 Ruins 27   ......㉞
13 Now 28   ......㉟
14 In the Field 29   ......㊱
15 Mold 30   ......㊴
16 Morning (3) 31   ......㊲

17	Beginning	32	……44
18	Mirror	33	……42
19	Expanse	34	……43
20	Concerning the Heart	35	……46
21	Song	36	……47
22	Concerning Shapes	37	……49
23	Clouds	38	……41
24	Dreams	39	……40

II

25	(In the midst of the world, I stir,)	42	……52
26	(A girl walks towards me.)	43	……53
27	(Earth is pregnant with a child of fire.)	44	……54
28	(When I try to sleep)	45	……55
29	(I'm copying down my memories.)	46	……56
30	(I won't let words rest.)	47	……57
31	(Sitting down in the world in a chair prepared for me,)	48	……58

32	(Occasionally time gives an undulating performance.) 49	59
33	(I started to get closer) 50	60
34	(Thanks to wind, trees know the joy of movement.) 51	61
35	(Returning from town) 52	62
36	(Because I looked too hard at the light) 53	64
37	(I go back into myself.) 54	65
38	(I lived,) 55	68
39	(Clouds fill up and dispose of themselves:) 56	69
40	(When I dream of where the distance finally arrives,) 57	70
41	(Gazing at the blueness of the sky) 58	71
42	(When the sky is seen through sunlight,) 59	74
43	(Here and there clouds were gathering) 60	75
44	(Because I was a fighter) 61	76
45	(In a fierce wind) 62	77
46	(The young sun briefly illumines) 63	79

47	(Time saturates the cloudy night sky.)	64	⋯⋯63
48	(We often hear the dark side of life)	65	⋯⋯88

III

49	(Who could know of my death)	68	⋯⋯82
50	(At times the stillness of existence)	69	⋯⋯84
51	(Even being here in this familiar scenery)	70	⋯⋯86
52	(As I stroll along this field,)	71	⋯⋯87
53	(In cloudy daytime, without shadows,)	72	⋯⋯83
54	(I unwittingly grew too separated)	73	⋯⋯85
55	(Just sitting around)	74	⋯⋯94
56	(Isn't the world one puny star within absence?)	75	⋯⋯96
57	(In the song I sing)	76	⋯⋯97
58	(Because of distance)	77	⋯⋯98
59	(Speaking worn-out words,)	78	⋯⋯92
60	(Just as wind rustles leaves of trees,)	79	⋯⋯95
61	(The heart softly touches the world.)	80	⋯⋯89

62	(Because the world loves me) 81	⑨¹

36 Unpublished Sonnets

1	Morning 84	①
2	Absence 85	②
3	(All you vain things!) 86	③
4	(Singing attacks death.) 87	④
5	(I was sleeping) 88	⑤
6	(Shouldering something —) 89	⑦
7	(Or possibly....?) 90	⑧
8	Today 91	⑩
9	(In the face of all things that kept silent) 92	⑪
10	(I searched my heart) 93	⑫
11	The Art of Night 94	⑬
12	Having Been Forgotten 95	⑭
13	(But there are things that are infinitely unknown) 96	⑯

14	A Noble Slap 97	⑱
15	Backtalk 98	⑲
16	Musical Accompaniment 99	㉑
17	Two Hearts 100	㉒
18	My Journeying 101	㉔
19	The Necessity of Greeting 102	㉕
20	A Factory 103	㉖
21	Once God.... 104	㉘
22	An Aphorism 105	㉙
23	Snow 106	㊳
24	(When I find myself in the casually changing afternoon-sunlight) 107	㊺
25	(People, when they have known unhappiness,) 108	㊽
26	(As I stroll along a modest street) 109	50
27	(The same sun and the same sky —) 110	51
28	(Birds peck at insects) 111	66
29	(I'm skipping) 112	67
30	(When I am apart from her) 113	72

31	(When I'm looking around the world) 114	73
32	(Something that comes) 115	78
33	(Something passed me like a smile.) 116	80
34	(It was towards the beginning of summer.) 117	81
35	(When, in darkness,) 118	90
36	(What small repose) 119	93

Afterword   120

[The Numbering of the Sonnets]

Tanikawa's original manuscript contains 98 sonnets in the fair copy. Each is numbered and some are titled. Out of these, 62 were selected and published as *62 Sonnets* in 1953, newly numbered. In the present book the original numbers of the 98 sonnets are given in the table of contents.

62 Sonnets + 36

Spring 1952 —— Autumn 1953

I

1   Shadows of Trees

And yet there is joy in this day
as in the heart of the young sun.
Of this joy the world of tables, guns and gods
is altogether unaware.

Only to this place
where people are standing
do shadows of trees lead their hearts home,
enveloped in this day's humility.

When I read the sky, sing of clouds,
or murmur in joy,
as in prayer,

sun and trees alike look upon
both what I've forgotten
and what I endlessly recall.

2 Longings

Under the shadow of the happy destiny of early
    summer sun,
my hopes neglected,
only my longings raced around
before I reflected on the vanity of things.

Knowing that fields and clouds are merely
    foolish,
how could I think that someone was enticing us
with all the lovely forms
I have loved without believing in?

Around my small grave, before long,
man, rock, and sky will remain.
But who can go on recalling tomorrow?

I've forgotten even God.
How could anything happen if I didn't live at all
under the shadow of the marvelously young
    destiny of early summer sun?

3   Homecoming

This was an alien land.
Opening the side door of this wretched earth,
I was attracted by the darkness inside,
by the deep and cryptic appearance of
    various rooms.

Who am I?
Not knowing how to go back home,
I keep on writing letters
about my finite sojourn here.

"I no longer aspire after other planets.
I will live on this planet with more pleasure
    than in eternity.
P.S. But even so someday I'll go home."

There may be an unexpected homecoming
from this familiar alien land —
a homecoming without me about which I
    know nothing.

4   Today

Sunday again, and
Monday again.
It's cloudy again and sunny again.
And who knows what's next?

Next? I have no idea.
There's only today.
There's no 'again' in me —
only 'today.'

I remember nothing but today.
Death would be 'today' and
living is intensely 'today.'

I love today
until a short song dies
and today is devoted to brief mourning.

5   Incidental Thoughts

So this is life after all?
People swarm the sun-swept morning streets;
children pass by, laughing like sparrows;
illusions whirl along like wind.

Today sings before eternity,
its song both younger
and more abstruse.
It sings more eternally than eternity.

In cities and villages, on deserts and seas,
talking goes on and on — amusing, awful
   and sad;
empty arguments rage and eyes burn day
   in and out.

So this is life after all?
Today this star is filled with so many
   cryptic things
that God is nearly forgotten.

6   Morning (1)

The overcast morning sky
conceals the night that has passed in thick
    clouds.
'So today has begun again',
whispers the young Hope.

I have no time or place to start from.
I live,
killing my days,
my heart alone overflowing.

I trust this overflowing heart;
trust its meaningless tears,
though I know nothing about serenity and
    assurance.

Morning is cloudy.
In the ubiquitous silence, night still lingering,
my heart, my poor puny heart, overflows.

7 Morning (2)

I was singing a morning meal,
painting the heart's liquid refreshment.
Are this-and-that linked
in this portent of a vast harmony?

Dressed in white, I woke up at light's delight
and the pangs of awakening
to feel and sing anew,
my heart no longer sleeping.

Death comes out of the earth, and
out of the future.
People die today and are left in ignorance.

But the heart must respond to every expanse.
The heart always starts to live
from here towards distant things.

8   Laughing

I wasn't either unhappy enough
to forget unhappiness
or happy enough
to forget happiness.

The sun kept speaking of day,
and the stars of night;
or say, rather, that a most beautiful silence
spoke of my heart and mine alone.

What is does not flow.
What comes and goes knows
nothing but this present moment.

To question the present moment is forbidden;
and one day, before this moment ends,
people may break out laughing.

9   Bewilderment

Society is nothing but
a human logjam;
and loneliness nothing
but one miserable specimen.

I'm bewildered.
Everything bewilders me —
politicians trying to employ me
when I'm employed by God,

and all other kinds of things;
a girl, catching a cold, philosophy.
And Fate wants to work in detail.

And so these lines of sonnets as a humble
    diversion.
No one will care what I say.
Will that make some fool think I'm a loner?

10   The Unknown

An automobile said,
so did a pencil
and chemistry:
'Man, you made me.'

What did a badger think about this?
What did the stars
and God think
of the foolish arrogance of this excessive passion?

Then let them die haphazardly one by one,
those who have forgotten what loneliness is:
'Here vanish the unknown.'

Wind blew over the earth at evening
    and over an unknown star.
God walked on the earth at evening,
and also on an unknown star.

11 Silence

Even when silence had given a name to
    everything
that my heart had welcomed,
suddenly I was frightened,
overcome by the awe of being unknown.

What words remain after the voice is lost?
What sort of heart beyond sadness?
And what sort of health is there between
    living and dying?
I started to whisper 'God,' but didn't.

It is always I who am responsible to talk
about myself, about the world,
knowing that I know nothing.

Not a word, not a voice,
no murmur, no song — not even a cough, yet
I have to talk about everything.

12 Ruins

No prayers of petition to God,
no philosophy to curse Him with;
if anything, there was only just
a faint song of God himself.

I shall never sing again
of yesterday's undoubted happiness,
of tomorrow with its dreary foreboding,
nor of today, skies clear to the point of vanity.

Ruins are the bones of time.
Just as today's wind blows towards oblivion,
the meaning of man vanishes into an utterly
 clear sky.

Ruins aspire only to keep standing
under the young sun —
to keep standing without meaning just for the
 sake of standing.

13 Now

Brilliance can illuminate anything.
Everything kindly forgets me
while I inhabit this moment
and love this moment unstintingly.

In a song that keeps ever silent
signs of God are faintly felt
and suddenly I am conscious of "now"
in this quiet sweep of space.

When I believe in the richness of this moment,
though I am aware of death on this planet,
I am free.

Passion can fill anything,
beneath whatever overflows and shines
    silently
such as the sun and the sky.

14 In the Field

My heart removed me to a height
from which I looked down on time.
I was remembered
and God's capriciousness glimpsed.

Without a song, without will,
today I'm just like a grade school boy eager to
    go home.
But who could possibly atone for what
on such a fine day as this?

People sing amiss.
They have no words to utter nothingness
and no words to utter everything.

But where I'm standing there is everything:
people on the street, grass in the field, and,
in the heavens, nothingness.   .

15 Mold

Clouds were roughly cast.
Distant mountains were trying to endure
    sunlight.
The landscape darkened over and cast
    shadows
that resembled the unevenness of my heart.

These were the mold of joy,
a negative space waiting for joy.
They could never become joy themselves.
They had to be filled in.

It's not sorrow that molds joy.
In the unknown, unfinished capriciousness
    of things
my heart received no name.

But once fulfilled and molded,
they will be completely forgotten —
the darkening landscape and my unnamed
    heart.

16 Morning (3)

The lamp was on all night.
A letter came at dawn.
The sky was lazy,
the children still asleep.

I get up,
throw things away,
pick up,
and get busy.

People start walking.
I begin to forget.
God starts weeping.

At nightfall everything will vanish.
I'm suddenly assailed by that premonition.
At that moment, all of a sudden, first light
    breaks.

17   Beginning

When there's no one,
a forgetful dream lives in me.
Time passes me by.
I smile wryly.

I escape;
but come too close again.
Touching the forms of terrible things
makes me conscious of a single heart.

Feigning ignorance,
I package time
and send it in the direction of yesterday.

Yet some things I can't abandon.
If I continue clinging to them
I find suddenly a new beginning.

18 Mirror

As I listen to the sounds of the heart
my own contours grow hazy.
When I have heart,
it is feeble unless it moves.

Everything is outside of me.
I try to enter the outside.
But the outside refuses me.
My heart wearies.

Inside of me there's only a thinking mirror.
My mirror is so docile
it reflects whatever it sees.

And things reflected are no longer existing
    things.
Gazing at the mirror, I try to get out.
My form within myself recedes but never
    vanishes.

19 Expanse

I keep on walking
through the expanse of things.
Suddenly the wind rises.
And time stirs.

Subtle gestures, though,
are soon forgotten.
In the expanse of which no one is aware,
time dies.

I will always be aware of an expanse beyond
　　human imagination.
I will learn to live and die
surrounded by things indifferent to me.

I keep on walking as if I, too, were a thing.
I stop looking.
And all at once I begin to live.

20 Concerning the Heart

Gradually I grew familiar with living.
Having believed till now only in shapes,
I've known nothing of the heart
and that made my solitude all the more cheerful.

Or rather maybe I was tired of the heart.
The resolute expanse of various shapes —
they "live" time and occupy space
more assuredly than the heart.

I have no song now.
I have a common origin with stars.
Whatever begot me had no heart.

But then suddenly the heart returns to me.
Is that because my shape is ugly?
No, rather because the shape of the world is
    too beautiful.

21 Song

When I looked up
the shapes of those clouds were already gone.
A heart familiar to me was
not in those fugitive shapes but outside of them.

Ancient prayers
continuously rain down curses on those shapes.
When heaven is vacant and earth holds a heart,
clouds, suspended, aspire to be something else.

But what could they become?
Softly, as though they hope to have hearts,
the clouds go on annihilating their own shapes.

There's so much of everything on earth
and so little in heaven
I seem to feel like singing.

22 Concerning Shapes

The presentiment of shapes
and the regret of shapes abound in the
    excessively clear sky,
although the shapes themselves are invisible,
like the heart.

Real shapes have no hearts.
It is shapes that are fugitive.
Besides, they fear ugliness
and extinction.

And yet my joy is in trusting in
and loving shapes;
or rather in trusting in a heart outside the
    shapes.

Today under this excessively clear sky
there is only one heart
and round about us only shapes are beautiful.

23 Clouds

Clouds were really beautiful this morning.
Though lacking hearts, they seemed
    illumined by one heart.
They accepted their own luminosity
and floated away like a momentary
    consolation.

I can believe in lots of things
and love them.
It's they that keep me living
and give me heart.

Human heart in its transiency
is hard to measure,
being too far or too near.

But trees live and people live,
assured of their time and place.
This morning I write a letter not addressed
    to the heart.

24 Dreams

For a moment, as if everything was a bright lie,
I was awake in my dreams.
I had no proof of anything.
I had only memories of happiness.

In the absence of some one,
today I trust too much in everything.
And suddenly a secret fear assails me,
when I have allowed myself even unhappiness.

A tree's shape.... the sea's shape.... the sun's....
I imagine someone in a landscape
whose shape is like that of a soul.

I have been too wide-awake.
I'll sleep undisturbed today
to prove the weight of my dreams.

II

25

In the midst of the world, I stir,
and the world, too, moves faintly.
As the world looks back,
celestial birds are startled and fly away.

The sky is suddenly empty.
Written words are too blinding.
I shade my eyes,
and only the distant mountains are clearly seen.

Time grows tired.
I don't know how to take care of it.
The heavens begin to assert themselves.

I keep on walking.
The world is watching me.
I turn my eyes away, towards death.

26

A girl walks towards me.
As we pass each other I am in love.
But distance is fast.
Oblivion overtakes her.

When I go shopping in the city
they give me my change in solitude.
I meander,
thinking how to use that change.

Of a sudden a flag signs the sky.
I throw up a particle of time at it
and that shatters the twilight.

I start to go home and forget how to walk.
Night begins luring me
but there are signs that tomorrow will bully me.

27

Earth is pregnant with a child of fire.
But, since no birth seems forthcoming,
clouds wish to be dabs of cotton for death.
And yet clouds weep too much for that.

The clock keeps complaining to time.
When time gets bored
even cats yawn.
I grow as lonely as an island.

By day, night is accused;
by night, day is accused.
I want to defend everything.

I casually stand up
and the world follows me.
I go into a toilet.

28

When I try to sleep
dreams get in my eyes.
Pain wakens me.
I measure philosophy's transparency.

Flowers carry on their own lives.
I touch a lot of lives as I stroll along.
My fingers gradually grow numb
and are finally frostbitten by death.

I dance
and kick everything away.
The world becomes a toy instrument.

I grow tired
and now I can sleep,
but can't forget how black the dreamless night.

29

I'm copying down my memories.
Old visions are all good ones.
The winter sunlight that warms my fingers
also falls across today's empty chair.

Between the window's outside and inside
a fragment of the world's picture is suspended.
As I reach to touch it
the beautiful thing gallops away.

I keep gazing at everything.
My heart reluctantly whispers
but love hushes it.

Today returns.
The back view of yesterday is already dark.
I can't imagine the shape of tomorrow.

30

I won't let words rest.
At times they feel ashamed of themselves
and want to die, inside of me.
When that happens I'm in love.

Among things that don't speak a word,
only people are loquacious.
What's more, sun and trees and clouds
are unconscious of their own beauty.

A fast-flying plane flies in the shape of a
    human passion.
Though the blue sky pretends to be a
    backdrop,
in fact there's nothing there.

I call out in a small voice.
The world doesn't answer.
My words are no different from those of
    the birds.

31

Sitting down in the world in a chair prepared
 for me,
I suddenly cease to be.
I shout,
and only words survive.

God has scattered false pigments across the
 heavens.
When we try to imitate the colors of the heavens,
both pictures and people die.
Trees alone stand strong against the heavens.

I bear witness in the midst of a festival.
I keep on singing
and happiness comes to measure my height.

I read a book of time.
Everything is recorded there, and therefore
 nothing.
I bombard yesterday with questions.

32

Occasionally time gives an undulating
    performance.
Meanwhile I store up fragments of eternity.
I measure my life's length.
I have a presentiment of things unknown.

The wind rises.
I plan a future based on memories.
The sun is high.
To live summer over again — my resolution!

Thus various regrets and various premonitions
build up inside of me.
As those age I shall grow intimate with death.

But today I'm still annoyed by the headache of
    being young.
It's like the labor that promises birth.
I start running; I have a life to waste.

33

I started to get closer
and backed off again.
I started to back off
and again drew near.

Always in utter self-forgetfulness
my mind gestures fantastically.
In trying to find the mind's order
I got lost in the human woods.

But I always have the joy of life as an excuse.
My love is leaping
so as at times to be indifferent to everything.

The blue sky is not a roof but an old well.
I throw myself in
only to be reborn.

34

Thanks to wind, trees know the joy of
 movement.
The sun, posing as a midwife,
looks conceited though it is young.
I smell the sun.

The music ends.
Life's weight permeates me.
I droop my head
and suddenly happiness peers into my face.

Since I've nothing to do with life
I just keep singing.
But I know how to praise.

When I at last reach the blue of the sky
there'll surely be no one there.
That sky is a benevolent lie.

35

Returning from town
I find silence nonchalantly occupying my room.
As I open the window without a word
I sense a black picture flowing in.

Under the streetlight's gaze
night's mutterings grow conspicuous.
Inside me are the pictures of the seasons.
Unlived in, they are extravagantly beautiful.

Voices come from far away,
calling no one
but merely thrown away towards the sky.

My daytime pupils aren't expanded yet.
Things in the dark are hard to distinguish
and only stars abound.

36

Because I looked too hard at the light
my shadow was as dark as night.
I calculate my loneliness
but there's no solution.

Once again all distances return to me.
I am familiar only with myself.
I've no place to dispose of my words.
I plot to convert them into sweat.

The heavens are forever a tedious stage setting.
Since everything is under them,
they become the measuring rod of distance.

Yet when I try to don sentimentality,
unfortunately I find the sleeves too short.
I recall my infancy.

37

I go back into myself.
No one's there.
Where do I come from?
I was born of infinity.

I'd like to be ubiquitous like light.
But what an insolent wish that is!
Song-like, my love is always thrown away,
unable to become even a mild breeze.

I go on living
and before long grow aware of love —
love, which I have nowhere to send, like nostalgia.

We have to use it up
in songs, in sweat,
or in other shapes of love.

38

I lived,
and the story became something that
    wouldn't end.
If we never forget,
aged gods can't sleep.

There's a midnight exchange
of tiny whispered words.
Midday songs are frozen
and over them whispers keep on sliding.

At the shrill cry of sinister birds,
the shapes of life
are sharpened in the silence.

I'm the story-teller.
The wind bears my ineloquence away.
When it has moved some distance away,
    I hear 'Love….'.

39

Clouds fill up and dispose of themselves:
why is that rain?
People dispose of their overflowing hearts:
why is that song?

The faint-hearted go on calling
the name of the world.
Yet trees don't reply.
Trees are too busy becoming the world.

When people realize they are part of an extension
they at once start talking tough; e.g.,
'I'm more important than trees.'

Thus, inaudibly, the trees whisper,
'It's important not to sing
but to empty your hearts.'

40

When I dream of where the distance finally
    arrives,
things at hand begin to murmur.
Because love goes strolling whimsically,
it always comes back perspiring.

Even running off to some forsaken place
and coming back hungry,
it has no lively place to call its own.
Night, as it has always been, is cold to
    lonely love.

As though in a changing of absences,
there's day and there's night.
And love cannot seek shelter there.

When I'm gone
the night that lingers is lovely,
and seems oblivious of me.

41

Gazing at the blueness of the sky
makes me feel I've a place to go back to.
But the brightness that has passed through
    clouds
no longer returns to the sky.

Sunlight everlastingly lavishly expends itself.
Even after dark, we are busy picking up its
    pieces.
Because people are all basely born
they don't rest as richly as trees.

The window contains what is overflowing.
I want no room except the universe.
So I am on bad terms with people.

To be is to injure space and time,
and the pain, if anything, reproaches me.
When I'm gone my health will return.

42

When the sky is seen through sunlight,
the color of nothing is beautiful.
To time's gentle questioning
I do not reply.

Bring me back yesterday morning!
For the vanished scenery
all I can do is
mourn.

Today, expectation looks like tomorrow.
But tomorrow,
expectation is nothing but today.

But one fine day is all around me.
Ever since childhood what pleasure have I
    had to live for?
Suddenly near at hand there are signs of
    something reviving.

43

Here and there clouds were gathering
the sky's overflowing light.
Wind whispers in my ear
and suddenly a great absence awakens.

Turning, I see someone.
I quietly leave my words behind.
That person treats them politely.
I sit on the world, as on a chair.

People gather
the sounds of the earth.
But there is no secret murmuring that will
 persuade me.

Yet sometimes among things that don't
 know me,
I sense a gusting happiness.
In that moment I have already returned.

44

Because I was a fighter
the blue sky was my shield
and I prowled the night.
I aimed at something beyond the world, but....

While my empty eyes roam around
I go on fighting, though there's no foe.
In the darkness I think I hear the world cough.
I brace myself.

But, unknown things inside and out of me
and how those are connected
make me dizzy.

My blood ebbs away.
I feel bound by dim memories.
I am no longer brave.

45

In a fierce wind
the earth is like someone's kite.
Even at high noon
people know that night is already there.

Because the wind has no language,
it can only run around fretfully.
I think of the wind on another star.
Could they possibly be friends?

The earth has night and day.
Meanwhile, what are other stars doing?
In what way do they endure expanding in silence?

In daytime the blue sky tells lies.
While the night is whispering truth, we are
    asleep.
In the morning everyone says he had a dream.

46

The young sun briefly illumines
my inner world that opens on the night.
Particles of dust are swarming in the sun.
Don't they foretell illness?

When did my feet ever steal from the earth,
as do the robust roots of trees?
When did I ever embrace the sky before praising
    the daylight,
as the young branches do?

It's silly to know the night.
The best I can do is leave sleeping things alone,
refraining even from singing gentle lullabies.

Everyone should keep silent at night.
We should ask nothing of the stars.
They don't even have cold laughter.

47

Time saturates the cloudy night sky.
When I stir, time falls over me like snowflakes.
My heart feels cold.
Only my blood is warm.

Things enjoyable by day hold their breath.
When I chase them they're no longer there.
Imaginary months and years fill my head.
I set them afire.

Memories burn.
Premonitions burn.
And today is left a heap of embers.

I can't believe in what really exists.
So I am given tomorrow in exchange for dreams.
When I awaken, the odors of breakfast are in
    the air.

48

We often hear the dark side of life
referred to solemnly:
graves, hearses, wills….
But these tell us nothing about death.

We who are living don't know beyond shadows.
We don't know what it's like to lose nothing.
We have too many mirrors.
So we're always peeping into life in reflection.

Soon, in death which has no mirrors,
we'll be spared being aware of ourselves.
We'll be able to be one with the world.

But in the rainy street today the living are
    busy living.
The evening paper reports suicides.
We're nothing but the distance that surrounds
    death.

III

49

Who could know of my death
in the midst of love?
Let me rather nurture desire in all its tenderness
so as to steal back the love of the world.

When I gaze at her,
the shape of life brings me back to the world.
A young tree and her figure
sometimes become one in me.

What I learn in touching her closed lips,
without naming the heart,
is carried away by a vast silence.

Yet in that moment I am also that silence.
And like a tree, I, too,
am stealing the love of the world.

50

At times the stillness of existence
is fainter than the stillness of nothingness.
Yet when we draw near
their subtle stirrings are revealed.

Don't they complain in their anxiety
about just being called
a tree, a cup,
a daughter, a picture....?

I know very well
about the certainty of existence. But
what can there be outside of people that we
    could name?

Nothingness is rather an easy thing.
Call as I will, the world doesn't waken.
All I can do is love foolishly.

51

Even being here in this familiar scenery
I find the world's richness bewildering.
I'd rather like to know everything that
    exists now
than what happened to things long ago.

The single-minded attitudes of things
    foredoomed to death
tempt me towards simple thoughts.
Only in this familiar moment
my thoughts are not inhibited by death.

Yet, in the silence of sky and sun,
this moment is constantly being taken away
and the pain of it suddenly scares me.

But I shall return into the world.
Has there ever been even one day without
    parting?
Into that world I return.

52

As I stroll along this field,
what kind of wind is blowing in that forest
while the sky with that cunning kindness
is hiding nothingness behind its back?

Every time I prepare to go home
something invariably escapes me.
I'm surrounded by absence
and grow tired sustaining it.

But for a while the sun indiscreetly illumines everything.
In such bare scenery
my shadow is blacker than night.

In that moment my absence is filled with trees, clouds and people.
My love bears them witness.
I begin instead to lean upon my absence.

53

In cloudy daytime, without shadows,
I watched words sicken.
My songs were sung by trees and grasses,
and my longings always came back down to earth.

Following the first ominous silence
we plunge pell-mell into a world of loquacity.
If words find their answers among people
they always fall ill apart from people.

I wish my words were as whole as those of the
    trees and grass
in that first silence
out of which everything was born.

What kinds of words are intimate with me?
Instead of myself singing
I hear myself being sung.

54

I unwittingly grew too separated
from the creatures whose birth is the same
   as mine.
I can no longer go back
among the earthly creatures.

But if we realized that even love is nothing
   more than our own possession,
who could keep from praying,
the more calmly because of that prayer's
   poverty,
that all might go on living?

I can possess nothing,
even though I love
trees, clouds and people.

I can only discard
my overflowing heart,
hesitant even to call that an act of love.

55

Just sitting around
I make my life bear fruit,
just as trees by keeping standing
participate in the vast circle of life.

That I may play sincerely
all the days allotted me
I just keep standing,
until my heart fails.

I am a discarded plate
in the shape of waiting,
knowing I'll never be filled.

And if I have in the world
a part to play,
my task is just standing like that.

56

Isn't the world one puny star within absence?
Twilight....
the world stands by idly,
as if ashamed of itself.

In such moments
I collect only little names
and some day
shall grow reticent.

Now and then sounds call the world,
more firmly than my song —
distant whistles, barking, the sounds of
    shutters and chopping.

In that moment the world is listening,
as breathlessly as twilight,
as if reaffirming itself sound by sound.

57

In the song I sing
the world is wounded.
I try to make the world sing
but it stays silent.

Words are
poor little kids forever lost.
Like dragonflies, they perch on things,
trembling in the midst of enormous silence.

They try to escape into things;
but words
cannot love the world.

They curse me and die,
snatched up by a star-bright sky.
— I sell their corpses.

58

Because of distance
a mountain can become a mountain.
Looked at too closely,
it resembles me.

Scenic panoramas stop people in their tracks,
making them conscious of enormous
    distances surrounding them.
Those very distances invariably
make people the people they are.

Yet people contain inside themselves
a distance.
That is why they go on yearning.

In the end people are just places violated
    by distances.
No longer observed,
people then become scenery.

59

Speaking worn-out words,
or rather no words,
and only having a heart capable of feeling,
I was content.

It has begun raining.
A girl comes running.
Ah, the wind....
These are already my songs.

Over and over, tirelessly,
I call the world's names;
the names of everything I love.

And even unhappiness,
as I continue praising it,
can become my foster-child.

60

Just as wind rustles leaves of trees,
the world ruffles my heart.
Though I speak of sadness sometimes,
    sometimes joy,
I can't name my heart correctly.

The world moves endlessly, expanding,
and I can never catch up.
I continue searching for my heart
in twilight or in rain or in cirrus clouds.

But sometimes I become equal to the world.
I yield myself
to wind, sunlight, seasons —

— I become the world
and lose song for the sake of love.
But I don't regret it.

61

The heart softly touches the world.
In that shape the heart continues nodding.
Now the wind rises.
Now a boy is running, and then

the heart again touches itself and
always returns to itself
one with the world,
in order to sing, even tentatively.

Who will catch my songs of praise?
It's better for joy to return to earth,
for then joy doesn't die in solitude.

You don't need to confess
love.
The world will see it in my eyes.

62

Because the world loves me
(now harshly,
now tenderly)
I can bear any length of solitude.

When I was first given someone to love
I listened to nothing but the world's sounds.
Only simple sorrow and joy are clear to me,
for I always belong to the world.

I throw myself into
sky, trees, people,
that I may soon become part of the world's
    richness.

....I call to her.
The world turns to me
and I vanish.

36 Unpublished Sonnets

1   Morning

The blue sky was already starting once again
above me and above all other people.
Light comes in the morning
for the first things.

I had no hope, no consolation and no peace
    of mind,
but my life was expanding.
Though there was nothing I knew,
I could call everything "joy".

Death came with no wisdom.
It didn't strike me as strange.
Even the forms of graves were full of empty
    meanings….

Everything was starting once again,
suffering over its ending,
just for the sake of starting without any
    proof or meaning.

2   Absence

Songs and the sky
support my heart.
And today I am absent in the winter sunlight,
a chair of happiness without me.

I was sitting in a dark universe without light.
I bought my tears in a department store and
    drank them
without the wisdom to name them
    "bitterness",
but just for the sake of futile things.

Today, too, I was forgetting all day long,
aware that I was forgetting,
among jostling small gods and demons.

Tomorrow, too, all day long....
But with no guarantee of not being lost
people wisely try to forget.

3

All you vain things!
Back me up!
Songs! Sky! Today!
Just back me up, without speaking your heart!

Both joy and sorrow are born from tears.
Nothing is crying before me
but laughter and anger are lost
when mountains and the sky are staring.

Once I enter myself through the eyes I can't
    get out of me,
on nights when my heart keeps endlessly
    murmuring,
on days when my heart keeps endlessly singing.

Who is it that live on the planet,
looking at all the faces,
knowing nothing about the heart?

4

Singing attacks death.
In daytime something fills and overflows,
and yet, the cradle has long since shaken off
the ever-impatient heart.

I am hungry for every day
and my heart is not wounded.
Yet my too obedient heart,
having been punished, has no hometown.

I have known the sky without flying
and my heart, having been punished by God
because praised by God,

has now forgotten serenity.
It has forgotten the names of happiness and
    unhappiness
in order to learn only to live.

5

I was sleeping
(What night was it?
What day was it?)
getting lost in an unfamiliar dream.

Coming? Going?
Or returning to a distant place?
I was dreaming, without walking,
with the enviable heart of an infant.

But I have so much yet to know,
as the light is born and dies,
that I don't even have time to weep.

When I have walked as far as the grave,
what will I ever notice
about the sun and the endless sky
    during the day?

6

Shouldering something —
that is the right destiny;
not giving off sparks, not moaning,
but just fulfilling each single moment —

thus moving alone in the dark universe
and fulfilling it,
hoping to find finally a bright meadow
but only after a lonely hundred years.

It wasn't a hundred years,
though today
my heart realizes that

to vanish
and be lost in the end —
that means to remain for ever and ever.

7

Or possibly....?
Then what are foolish things?
Light lives, light dies
and trees say nothing about that.

Saying nothing about enduring,
leaving everything as it is,
feeling that that's all there is,
in calm wisdom,

trees, rather, are brimming from their depths,
ever since primitive times,
for no one's sake,

wisely accepting what there is as it is,
and things they don't know about
as they are living.

8 Today

Compensated—
on a quiet snowy night
by beauty that is white only and unknown,
white upon futile things.

Growing intensely old,
having no earth,
you, heavy dream, sank into the pond of time,
as did your dread!

But it will not end.
Hoping in summer
and repenting in autumn

today and again today,
as if it were a cold time,
as if it were a cold place....

9

In the face of all things that kept silent
only my heart was anxious to listen.
In the face of all things which were only faces
only my heart was looking for its companion.

Someone is certainly singing,
besides his pitiful phantom.
But his heart wore
its own smile.

"During the hundred years when I'll have to
 give up,
I will die, never giving up,
aware even of death."

So sang
my heart about itself
in the face of all things that don't answer.

10

I searched my heart
in my phantasma.
The day asked me numerous questions till it
   got dark
and at night I waited in silence for someone
   to name me.

Who asks and who gives a name?
And who calls his own heart heavy?
Those who kept silent were strong.
Those who knew nothing were strong. But

I know
one heart, and
such a weight as of today.

When someone to be named has died
and in spite of that knowledge I keep silent,
the heart will be lost.

11   The Art of Night

Festivities in the sky,
mourning on earth, people say.
But then who is it that curses
with that swift art of night?

The running and striking day sleeps
and the thinking day doesn't sleep.
Disease watches and
night wakes up.

The sun told the meaning of the stars
and the stars told the heart of the sun.
Keeping them at arm's length, I listened.

And then the sky fell silent.
We should offer ourselves before we
    question and fall ill,
knowing that a single heart is itself the
    whole heart.

12 Having Been Forgotten

What *is* so-and-so
is later said to have been so-and-so,
but what *was* so-and-so
can only live in what *is* so-and-so.

One said, "Happy"
and the other said, "Unhappy"
(and about what?)
without regretting the folly of their ignorance.

Onto hand and heart that try to repeat
    themselves
foliage swirls down, and snow falls white
    and just,
but no longer in one's memory.

After "now" in which people live and which
    is infinite
even time will dwell in Heaven,
but no longer remembered.

13

But there are things that are infinitely unknown
in fields, on the streets, within me, and yet
I must move along
so that my heart will not weep.

Always putting an end to living
and starting to live;
shouldering the heart
and intensely trying to give it up,

with the heart as arms and tears as sweat,
letting yesterday go and letting tomorrow go,
I must move along by myself,

throwing away my dried-up will
to the unknown eerie earth and sky,
until suddenly today turns into a dark memory.

14 A Noble Slap

Someone's back departing
makes me impatient even in a dream.
There is a fool who thinks at midday
if only he knew how to pray.

Who will remain?
Who will vanish and go away?
In planning reincarnation from star to star,
busy God makes a mistake.

Who swims fastest?
Such a drummer as Asura!
A great poet who takes ten years for three lines!

Cowardly scoundrels continue waiting
for a noble slap
of absurd passion valid only for today.

15 Backtalk

Now I am a man.
Within me who put on airs,
"hope" that resembles me who have grown up
has timidly begun to write something called
    poetry.

Now I am a man.
Now no one can give me anything.
Now I have already perceived
what living is and how phony it is.

But good God says,
"Just live. It's not so bad."
He pats me on the shoulder too familiarly.

I talk back to Him because I'm already a
    grown-up,
"Charter a train for my requiem
or leave everything to me."

16 Musical Accompaniment

People sing.
Of what? Of some eternally mysterious thing.
So the sad tune of the bugle is singing
a distant thought of which people are unaware.

How pitiful and silly the brave tune sounds!
Hearing the vain bravery of the musical
  accompaniment
played as if a serious game,
Martians or the people of some other planet
  frown.

Coming down from a single cell via apes,
when did we ever notice something mysterious?
The cold profiles of galaxies and nebulae!

What else is there besides the intimate earth?
What else besides intimate today?
Nevertheless we still wage war with
  accompaniment!

17 Two Hearts

Late at night I hear
frogs singing.
Late at night I hear
sirens wailing.

The two hearts are in themselves
too difficult to understand.
Yet something sad appeals to us
who live more vigorously.

Did people ever understand?
Or did everything exist in the beginning?
Our sins which we fearlessly wear out....

Late at night I didn't meet any of God's agents
but I feel I am myself God's agent.
If so, would people call me a traitor?

18 My Journeying

There are stories close to me
and stories distant from me,
in a music which, foretelling my life,
comes back to me.

Fascinated by distant scenery and things,
I travel through my heart.
Young mysteries have all been inhabited....
But on a new earth

I should have a bird's-eye view of the stars
and live again on the earth
believing in answers from summer, sky and sun.

A story for each of us....
Someday someone will sing it
beneath Earth where there's nothing but
    peace of mind.

19 The Necessity of Greeting

My ruler is vast.
Farther than two billion light-years
my question reverberates,
nightly in the hollow hundred years.

Could I really be a human being?
Suspended in the nebulae and vacuum,
reluctantly toying with meanings,
I eat breakfast.

Small happiness dwelling in
large unhappiness
can no longer control the heart.

So I'll go out into the street and ask by way
    of greeting,
"Could I really be a human being?"
to confirm the real heart of the sun by
    treading on the earth.

20   A Factory

Someone manufactured things,
which everyone would use.
It was a noble assembly line,
though details about casualties are not known.

The grass used green.
Humans used love.
The sky used longing.
And I — used the heart.

It's been a century's waste.
No. It's been passion burning up everything.
Who should bear the blame for complaints?

Finally the factory went bankrupt
and manufactured simpler things such as algae.
Even years grew old.

21 Once God....

The vacuum dimly remembered
that there was once God.
It murmured almost inaudibly
that long ago God created me.

A delightful and quiet breakfast—
is that out of a mere habit of God's?
There's no one and there's nothing—
is that one of the rules?

The coldness of what remains after death—
other people's eyes, the desert's mask and
the sun, moon and stars without me—

How far and till when will I be able to walk
after stamping out the smoldering embers
    of God's bonfire,
devising new matches....?

22 An Aphorism

Stars shed their leaves in the dark night
and a child knows in the morning it's autumn.
Scholars look down
and calculate vain thing:

"Who is in stones, for example,
God or bacteria?"
So four seasons tirelessly keep on murmuring
and people go on dying, saying to themselves
  "O, my God!"

"Some day a gorgeous horizon will open before
    you
and surely a splendid truth will shine" —
so saying, many a sad fairy tale misled boys
    and girls.

But now God is an aphorism.
Soiled by the grime of irritation
God is worn away day after day.

23 Snow

The meaning of a path
is up in the deep snow on a plateau,
the meaning of a path leading up to the sky,
resembling a dream dreamed by an old tree.

Let today
bear the sky on its back
so that yesterday's footprints
may forget tomorrow's path.

Who is it walking along the mountain ridge
 singing,
trying to grasp the clouds together with his own
 sadness,
standing on tiptoes today in snow white and deep?

When people's new spring disperses the snow
and just an ordinary frozen corpse is discovered,
the meaning of the path which was true for an
 individual will be lost.

24

When I find myself in the casually changing
 afternoon-sunlight
I suddenly feel the chill of living.
When I place myself in idleness in which
 nothing happens
the shape of living is serene and even brighter.

There are times when one loses all of one's
 hometowns—
when, failing to find them across the mountains,
 beyond the clouds, amid people,
one returns again to one's own self;
when one finds people too poor to call oneself
 one's own hometown.

People then abandon the words, 'Go home'
and just live,
just live here and now—

Winter sunlight teaches me that
I am young nevertheless.
I continue believing in something more
 beautiful than resignation.

25

People, when they have known unhappiness,
become for the first time aware of happiness.
But because I know too much happiness
I have always been aware of unhappiness.

How sad nights are!
They sleep between the stars.
How sad days are!
They always shine in vain to destroy shadows.

And how sad lives are!
Uncertain about happiness or unhappiness,
they count their small days.

Only unaware people are happy.
When I become aware of happiness and
    unhappiness,
sad indolence becomes mine.

26

As I stroll along a modest street
I see more and more intimate things that I can
    say hello to.
When I'm singing small little songs
the happiness as I sing is my own.

While we are alive
only death deserves to be called true
    unhappiness.
Even being wounded is pleasant to me, still
    young,
when pain itself is the proof of my living.

To me every single day is irreplaceable.
I wish such days would stay awake forever
expanding quietly but with certainty.

Finally, at the moment of my death
those days will turn out to be my grave,
still as heavy as I could believe them to have
    been.

27

The same sun and the same sky—
these make remembrance trustworthy:
this quiet expanse left in me
by the days I have so far lived through.

Various things,
disguised as the happiness of those days,
are waiting for me to turn back to them
unafraid of committing the sin of forgetting today.

Nostalgic shapes pass through me.
In that plain landscape
there remains the distance that has died away.

Soon, today turns into an old illusion.
But every time it does
things keep piling up in me.

28

Birds peck at insects
joyfully.
The blue sky spreads above them
joyfully.

I, too, hide my small happiness
because my unhappiness gets jealous.
I kick a stone
and the uneven surface of a planet comes to mind.

Soon I shall gamble a little
on a lovely future.
When I lose, I'll have forgotten about the gambling.

But who is this expressionless boss of the gaming table?
I'll throw the birds at him,
who dominates happiness.

29

I'm skipping
on flowery patterns.
But sometimes I stumble
and the patterns become assertive.

I am obliged to respect existing things.
Humbling myself,
I looked at the exhibition of God's works.
I even bought some of them.

Everything costs almost nothing.
Even my birth is inexpensive.
True value can be bought for nothing.

At the end I have only to pay myself.
But it's essential that I grow fat by then
to make it known that I ever existed.

30

When I am apart from her
she is walking somewhere I don't know.
When I look too hard
suddenly she and I both disappear.

If she walks within my solitude
I become even lonelier.
When she is walking alone
I love her in the world.

When our eyes meet
we are reminded of each other.
The world then turns into a dream.

But she doesn't stare.
I'm constantly worried.
So I don't stare either.

31

When I'm looking around the world
I happen to see her from the back.
I try to prevent her
from escaping.

Even the girl I know
is to me just a stranger.
But if I touch the fingers I know,
all of a sudden she becomes dear to me.

There is an expanse she knows.
The wind blows.
There is an expanse I know.

When she happens to peek at herself
I notice how cold her fingers are.
Suddenly I begin to love.

32

Something that comes
and goes
like quiet love
always attracts my heart.

Is living, too, something like this,
without our knowing where it comes from
and where it will go,
disguised as a transient happiness?

I trust in Earth's happiness;
in violent things
and even more in humble things.

I resemble a tree.
Silently
I continue being given to by Earth.

33

Something passed me like a smile.
But did it happen last year?
Kind people have disappeared from my room
and now it's occupied only by small yet
    impudent time and space.

Wry smiles remain in relief on the wall,
while my heart is looking out the window as if
    nothing had happened.
But I live in my room
and the blue sky is painfully unchanged.

But did this and that also happen last year?
Somehow things are easily forgotten now
and I always have only "tonight" that resembles
    "last night".

Yes, I'll say, for instance,
"Time continuously steals my *now*", or
"Last night is no longer my night."

1952. 7

34

It was towards the beginning of summer.
While constantly ending,
it wounded me,
but was painfully true.

I can't call it a small parting.
Like too serious a boy,
the moment of truth always stares at me
asking me to repent.

Why was I not satisfied with transient joys—
sky, wind, leaves rustling and
my ever-aspiring heart?

But it was towards the beginning of summer
that I rued the time
and sought for a heart outside of myself.

1952. 7

35

When, in darkness,
nothing remains with me but memories,
I am like a gravestone devoted to remembrances,
surrounded by dark flowers.

Those things that used to move about so
    vigorously
are now confined to an obstinate oldness,
described completely in a few words,
with a kind of uncertainty no longer palpable.

How precious those countless small things were
that I carelessly threw away in my life!
No one remembers that now.

Sunlight illuminates today in cruel brightness.
But memories are now twilight which will never
    awaken.
Like sin, they have no place to return to.

36

What small repose
will remain for me
when finally
I have forgotten sorrow and joy?

Only the faint remembrance of the vast expanse
is settling within me like a presentiment of
    which I have repented.
In an unfamiliar dream I count intimate things
    one by one.
But when I have gathered them all I've already
    forgotten everything.

I am like that monument-maker who polishes
    gravestones all day long.
He keeps on polishing a small memento of one life.
He always sees himself reflected in the gravestone
    that shines every moment.

But there is no proof there.
Rather, in continuously working
he finds some small consolation.

Afterword

The ninety-eight poems included here are all written in the same pattern and I called them 'sonnets' after the European verse form. They were written between April 1952 and August 1953, out of which sixty-two were selected and published as *62 Sonnets* by Tokyo Sogensha in 1953; and then in March 2001, with one unpublished 'sonnet' added, Kodansha republished it as one of the "+α Library" series and so the present volume is the third publication.

It is delightful but also seems to me unbelievable that poems I started writing in my twenties are still being read half-a-century on. I think they might have some merit of which the author himself is unaware. So I decided this time to have all of the ninety-eight 'sonnets' published along with English translations.

In a 1957 essay I wrote: "*62 Sonnets* is a book of my youth. I can say without hesitation that I was a typical youth and was faithful to my own youth. ….The book is, broadly speaking, a song in praise of life." As I think back on it now, it is just as I said. When I heard Kawamura, one of the translators, who is knowledgeable about English verse, say, "Translating

these poems is a hard job but is all the more delightful for that," it occurred to me that the language that made these poems possible came from a deeper stratum of consciousness than the surface, and that this might be the source of a certain musicality which arises from among the words and is part of the charm of these poems.

In other words, these poems are apt to incline, in terms of language, toward ambiguity and vagueness, and consequently they prove difficult for the reader. But poetry is apprehended not by the brain's left hemisphere alone. For the appreciation of poetry, the difficult function of verbalization by the right hemisphere is also indispensable. By reading these poems in both Japanese and English—each language presenting its own unique set of implications—one's appreciation of poetry might turn out differently. Anyway the author wishes that there would be no great gap between the youth of fifty years ago and the youth of the twenty-first century.

Shuntaro Tanikawa
June 2009

集英社文庫

62のソネット＋36
62 Sonnets＋36

2009年7月25日　第1刷　　　　　　　　　　定価はカバーに表示してあります。
2024年12月18日　第3刷

著　者　谷川俊太郎
　　　　たにかわしゅんたろう
訳　者　Ｗ・Ｉ・エリオット
　　　　かわむらかずお
　　　　川村和夫
発行者　樋口尚也
発行所　株式会社　集英社
　　　　東京都千代田区一ツ橋2-5-10　〒101-8050
　　　　電話　【編集部】03-3230-6095
　　　　　　　【読者係】03-3230-6080
　　　　　　　【販売部】03-3230-6393（書店専用）
印　刷　株式会社広済堂ネクスト
製　本　株式会社広済堂ネクスト

フォーマットデザイン　アリヤマデザインストア　　　　マークデザイン　居山浩二

本書の一部あるいは全部を無断で複写・複製することは、法律で認められた場合を除き、著作権の侵害となります。また、業者など、読者本人以外による本書のデジタル化は、いかなる場合でも一切認められませんのでご注意下さい。

造本には十分注意しておりますが、印刷・製本など製造上の不備がありましたら、お手数ですが小社「読者係」までご連絡下さい。古書店、フリマアプリ、オークションサイト等で入手されたものは対応いたしかねますのでご了承下さい。

© Shuntaro Tanikawa/W. I. Elliott/Kazuo Kawamura 2009
Printed in Japan　　ISBN978-4-08-746459-7　C0192